Lock Down Publications and Ca$h
Presents

I0658218

Countdown of a Killa 2

Sick With Greed

Written By

Lo-Life

First Edition 2025

Printed in the United States of America

Lock Down Publications
P.O. Box 944
Stockbridge, GA 30281
www.lockdownpublications.com

Like our page on Facebook: Lock Down Publications
www.facebook.com/lockdownpublications.ldp

Stay Connected with Us!

Text **LOCKDOWN** to 22828 to stay up-to-date with new releases, sneak peaks, contests and more…

Like our page on Facebook:
Lock Down Publications

Join Lock Down Publications/The New Era Reading Group

Visit our website:
www.lockdownpublications.com

Follow us on Instagram:
Lock Down Publications

Email Us: We want to hear from you!

Prologue

When she pulled up to the house, she couldn't believe what her eyes were seeing. Immediately, jealousy reared its ugly head. The house was beautiful. The lawn was well manicured. The neighborhood seemed quiet and peaceful.

Meme couldn't understand how Ty could afford to buy a house, cash! Something wasn't adding up. She hopped out and rang the bell.

Minutes later, a sexy but obviously young man answered the door. Clad in a pair of grey joggers and a beater, his muscles were bulging. Meme couldn't help but sneak a peek at his dick print. "Can I help you?" Marcus asked.

"I'm looking for Shatyra. Is she home?"

"Oh, no. She's not here right now."

"Aunt Meme!" Little CJ screamed with joy. His little self couldn't contain his excitement. He ran to the door to greet her.

"Heyy, Pooh Bear. What's been up?" She grabbed him into a hug.

"Nothing. We moved."

"I see that. Where's your momma at?"

"She left. She'll be back in a little bit," he informed her. Seeing the familiarity between the two, Marcus offered Meme to come in. Once inside, she could tell the house was scarcely furnished.

"Oh. I'm Meme by the way. Ty and I have been best friends for most of our lives. We're practically sisters," she claimed, neglecting to mention her and Ty hadn't talked in months.

"I'm Marcus. I'm just a friend of the family." *A friend of the family, my ass!* In Meme's mind, Ty had a little boy toy she was shacking up with. Meme checked him over once more and felt she may need to get a sample of what he had in the joggers, one of these days.

CJ offered to give her the tour. She reluctantly allowed him to lead the way. What Meme wanted was to learn more about the mysterious Marcus. What was his role in Ty acquiring the new house?

After about forty-five minutes, Meme decided it was time to go. Plus, Ty hadn't come back, and she wasn't quite sure of what her reaction would be. Meme figured, she'd try and catch up to Ty on another day. Maybe on neutral ground. One on one!

"Aunty, can you take a picture . . . so I can send it to my daddy?" CJ asked. Meme had totally forgotten about Bo. It seemed like everybody did. Well, except his only son. Meme wondered what Bo had been up to. She'd heard he was messing with homosexuals now. If he was to win his appeal, she definitely wasn't letting him get up in her goodies any longer.

"Sure, thing, Pooh Bear. She sat with him on the couch and proceeded to take selfies. She noticed Marcus was in a couple of the frames. He was talking idly on his cell phone in the kitchen. She didn't know why, but something told her she needed to make sure he was in the picture also.

After taking three different shots, she told CJ she would get them developed and bring them back, so he could send them to his daddy.

Two weeks later, CJ was playing on his miniature basketball goal in the front yard. Ty was in the kitchen cooking. Marcus left to go to the grocery store and Mya was at her *friends'* house, yet again.

A black sedan turned on their street and crept to a stop, twenty feet away from their front door. Parked in front of a blue and white house. For ten minutes, no one emerged from the vehicle. It just sat there, idly waiting. *Watching.*

CJ missed a rebound. The ball ricocheted off the curb and rolled down the street, stopping three feet away from the black sedan. Just as CJ walked up to grab the ball, the front passenger door opened. He jumped, startled. Then, recognition sat in. After a small conversation, CJ hopped inside the car, and was never seen or heard from, again.

Thirty minutes after CJ left, Marcus turned down their street. He noticed CJ's basketball; it had traveled halfway down the road. He stopped the car, scooped it up and continued to the house. Once he walked in with the groceries, he called out to CJ. No answer. *Maybe he went upstairs.*

He found Ty cooking chicken in the kitchen. "Here goes the rest of what you needed," he told her as he gave her a kiss on the cheek.

"Baby. Can you tell CJ to come in, so he can get ready for dinner?"

Marcus looked at Ty confused. "What do you mean? He's already inside the house."

"Huh? Baby, I would know if he came into the house." Realization hit. She ran outside yelling his name. "CJ! CJ! Baby, where are you?" They searched everywhere. Even places they knew he would never go. Just as they both concluded, something horrible had occurred, Ty received a call from a private number. "Hello?"

"We have your son. We want two hundred and fifty thousand dollars by the end of the week, or he's dead. If you go to the cops, then he's dead. This is sudden death. Clock's ticking." The caller hung up. Ty's whole body crumbled. She collapsed on the floor, crying for her baby boy and asking God why her, why always her?

Chapter 1

Three Days Prior:

Meme just left Ty's house feeling envious. She just couldn't understand how broke ass Ty could afford a big ass house in such a nice ass neighborhood. *It has to be the young nigga.*

She knew one thing. She needed to get to the bottom of it. If Ty could do it, she knew for sure, she could. She made a left down her street. Her phone began to ring. The ring tone was very familiar and long awaited. Meme frantically rummaged through her purse, trying desperately to locate her phone. Finally, she pulled it out and answered. "Hello?"

"Wassup, baby girl. You miss me?" She couldn't contain her smile. Just hearing Pat's voice gave her chills.

"Of course I've missed you. You've been having me going crazy out here," Meme admitted.

Pat chuckled. "Well. You wanna come show me how much you've missed me?" Pat asked seductively, his hand gripping his dick as he talked to her.

Meme bit her bottom lip. "Where you at?" She was ready to travel to hell if need be. Just to get her a taste of Pat.

"I'm at my crib. My old lady's here, but she's about to go to her momma's house on the southside. She'll be gone until tomorrow night. Her mom's sick, so she cooks and cleans for her. So, I need someone to come take care of me. Tonight."

That was music to her ears. "Let me head to the crib real quick. Imma grab some overnight clothes, and then I'm on the way."

"Bet!" Meme was so excited, she wanted to stop the car, hop out and twerk on her headlights. She pulled up to her apartment. Her boyfriend—Slick—was parked in her normal parking spot. She grimaced.

Her and Slick had been messing around for a couple years now. They'd met at the club one night, hit it off, and have been a couple ever since. Of course, being that Slick was from another side of town, he had no idea how much of a stain Meme had on her reputation. By the time he started hearing about her exploits, he was already in too deep. *Head over heels.*

Meme had love for Slick, but he was one of those types of dudes who seemed to never be able to get it right. Sometimes, it seemed as if he was hustling backwards. One day, he'd have ten bands on him. The next week, he'd have to borrow ten dollars. His dick was good, but Meme knew a good dick didn't necessarily pay the bills unless the nigga that was attached to it was selling it. Even though she wouldn't have minded, Slick was giving his dick away. For *free.*

Now, she had to figure out how she was going to shake him for the night. Meme hopped out of the car and walked through the breezeway. One of her little side boos named Lil Pauly was posted up, serving a fiend. He saw her approaching, grabbed at his dick and bit his bottom lip. "Damn, Meme. When you gon' let a nigga get up in them guts again?" The yellow shorts Meme had on were digging all up into her coochie. He couldn't keep his eyes off her camel toe.

Lil Pauly was a brown-skinned, twenty-two-year-old stocky dude, who grew up with Meme's younger brother, Mayo. One day, she came home drunk from the club. After stumbling upon Pauly late night hustling, they had a short back and forth conversation. Five minutes later, he had her pinned up against the wall in the breezeway. Her back against the bricks. Her thighs sitting on his shoulders, as he feasted on her box. Out in the open, where anyone could walk up and catch them in the act.

"It all depends, Pauly . . . You gon' hit a bitch pockets?" Meme was all about her bottom line. She loves dick, but she worshiped the almighty dollar.

"You know I ain't trippin 'bout blessing your game. You from the hood. Day one! Just let me know when we can link up," Pauly told her. Meme made sure she let her hand graze the front of his pants, as she walked by. She heard him say, "Meme. You hell." She turned the corner, headed to her apartment door. She stood at the door for a few seconds, took a deep breath and walked in.

As soon as she stepped in, weed smoke smacked her against her face. Her apartment looked as if a hurricane hit it. Clothes were scattered all over the floor. A half opened pizza box sat on the coffee table. Slick and his homeboy—Tator—sat playing 2K, as if they weren't thirty years old and broke. "Heyy, baby," he called out, not once taking his eyes off the screen. Meme grunted in response. She walked by, headed to her bedroom.

She quickly undressed, hopped in the shower and scrubbed herself thoroughly. Meme contemplated on whether or not to even give Slick the dignity of lying to him. At the end of the day, it was nothing that would stop her from heading over to Pat's to spend the night. She was going to give him some of her good loving. No matter what!

Meme hopped out of the shower, threw on some white tights and a pink wife beater. She slipped on a pair of pink and white Dunks, pulled on a PINK hoodie, and grabbed her keys. After snatching her purse, she was headed right back out the door. As the door shut behind her, she heard Slick call out. "Baby. If you going to the store, pick me up a . . ."

She was so sick of Slick and his bum ass ways. That's why she was so hell-bent on locking down a boss nigga. Someone who could take her out the hood. Put her in a house like Ty's. *No, fuck that!* Bigger than Ty's.

Meme got directions from Pat, then made her way to him. She contemplated stopping to get some condoms. But then, she thought better of it. If he wanted to buss up in her, so be it. Hopefully, she would get pregnant. She had three abortions in the past. If she were to get pregnant, it would surely be a blessing.

Just as she pulled up to his crib, Slick started blowing her phone up. "You just gon' have to be mad, boo boo," she whispered to the phone, as she powered it off.

Pat answered the door on crutches. He had a cast over his left leg. The lacerations on his face were barely healed properly. Yet, he looked so handsome to Meme. She gave him a loving and tender hug. "Heyy, baby. How you feeling?" She cooed.

"I'm good. But I'm way better now," he countered. They walked in and took a seat on the couch in the living room. Pat flipped through his HULU app and found a movie to watch. He leaned back, his broken leg on the floor, his head resting on the armrest. Meme leaned back into him, both of them laughing at Madea.

Meme kept feeling his dick poking her in her lower back. "Damn. I'm glad to see I can still make that motherfucka rise," she purred. She reached into his shorts, fishing out his semi-erect cock.

"I bet you can still make it spit up too," he challenged. Meme giggled and took him into her mouth.

"Ssshhiittttt!" Pat hissed, as the tip of his dick scraped the back of her throat. Meme trapped his rod between her lips, held him there, while she worked his shorts down his thighs. "Hold up. Let me get the camera," he said. Meme hesitated for a split second, before she gave in.

She popped him out of her mouth. "Use mine. Just in case your girl goes snooping in your phone. You can always send it to your email." She grabbed her purse, powered her phone back on, unlocked it and handed it to him.

Once he confirmed he had the camera recording, Meme went back to eating his dick and balls. Now that she knew she was being recorded, she became extra nasty with it. She gobbled him up, as if her life depended on it. *Ghlup. Ghlup. Ghlup.* Spit covered her fingers, cascading over his balls.

Every so often, she'd look into the phone. Let the viewer know she was *that* bitch. "Agghhh, shit. I'm cumming, bitch. Get all that shit, baby." Pat gripped the side of her head tightly, jerked, and spurts of gooey cum spewed into her mouth.

Meme allowed it to pool on her tongue. She opened her mouth, showed the world, then swallowed the whole load in one gulp. "Damn, girl. Whooh. A nigga missed your ass!" Pat confessed, breathlessly.

Meme kissed the tip of his dick head. "You better have," she playfully said, getting up to go brush her teeth. While she was gone, Pat decided to go ahead and send the video to his email. As he scrolled through her gallery, something caught his attention. His face instantly began to sour.

His heartbeat quickened. His blood boiled. He stared at the picture of Meme and a little boy. In the background, the face of a man he would never forget. A man he thought he would never see again. The man that ran him off the road, robbed him, then left him for dead.

Now, he was looking at Meme sideways. *Is she down with this nigga? Is this all some game she's playing, just to get close to me, so he could rob me again?* He hated the fact that he was banged up. Plus, his pistol was all the way upstairs.

If ole boy ran up in his crib right now, Pat would be a goner. He frantically searched for a weapon. He grabbed his crutches and hopped into the kitchen. After snatching up a butcher's knife, he went back into the living room. He sat down and waited for Meme to return.

Moments later, she appeared, wearing nothing but her pink and white, French-cut, laced panties and her wife beater. Nipples poking. Areolae, dark and lovely behind the cotton fabric. She hadn't picked up on Pat's discerning demeanor.

Meme laid back against his chest. He draped his right arm over her chest. His left hand gripped the knife discreetly. Meme saw her phone on the coffee table, picked it up and viewed the video herself.

Once it was over, she went to put the phone back down, when Pat suddenly grabbed her by her chin, yanking her head back; the blade's sharp point pricking at the flesh of her neck. "Oh my God! Oh my God," she struggled to say.

"Who's that nigga that robbed me?" Pat growled into her ear, menace dripping off each syllable.

"Robbed? Baby, I swear, I don't know what you're talking 'bout. Your nephew said that you were in a car accident." Meme pleaded.

"Bitch. You're lying!" Pat screamed. A small trickle of blood dripped down her neck. She trembled in terror.

"Baby. I swear, on my momma and my granny, I don't know what you're talking 'bout."

"Go to your pictures," he ordered.

"Huh?"

"In your phone. Go to your pictures' gallery," he insisted. She did as told. Once she scrolled over the picture, he yelled, "Stop! Who is that?" He was referring to Marcus.

Meme was confused at the accusation. "Pat, I don't know that nigga. That lil boy is Ty's son. The nigga's somebody she's fucking with. I just met him for the first time that day. I swear on my life," she begged. Tears began to fall rapidly. Meme didn't want to die. Especially, for something she had nothing to do with. The fact Pat thought she had anything to do with him getting robbed hurt her deeply.

Pat sat and analyzed. His gut was telling him she was being honest. He needed to make sure her loyalty belonged to him. "Okay. Okay. Well, if you're telling the truth, that means you'll help me get back what's rightfully mine, right?" he asked her devilishly.

"Of course, baby. Whatever I need to do, I'll do it." She was happy and eager to help right the wrong.

"I need you to help me get that lil boy. Asap!" Meme's heart broke. She'd been in little CJ's life, his entire existence. She knew, if Pat wanted the little boy, it wasn't for anything good. But, what choice did she have? If she didn't agree, Pat would think she was guilty of setting him up.

"Okay, baby. I got you. I'll get him," Meme assured him.

"That nigga took two hundred and fifty thousand dollars from me," Pat lied. "When I get that back, I'll give the kid back," he claimed. All she could do was nod. Too afraid to voice herself. Pat lowered the blade and kissed the top of her head. She still trembled in his embrace. He informed her that she would do the deed with one of his most trusted soldiers. Now, she knew the who, what, why. Only thing left was the when. He eventually told her.

Present Day:

Marcus crouched over Ty as she laid on her kitchen floor. Bawling her eyes out. Curled in the fetal position. "Not my baby boy!" she howled. He tried to console her, but Ty was lost to her agony. Her cell phone laid beside her, cracked from the fall when she got the dreadful call.

How could CJ have gotten kidnapped in the front yard like that? Marcus couldn't understand. He'd just left for the store, thirty minutes before. Ty cried herself tired in his arms. Afterwards, they sat and discussed the game plan. "You said they want two hundred and fifty thousand dollars?"

"Yeah. That's what the kidnappers said. So, I got a week."

"No, *we* got a week. Look, I got like ninety stacks upstairs. So really, we have like six days to come up with sixty bands. We can do it. We've done it before. That's only an average of ten bands a day. We should be able to do that in our sleep," Marcus boasted, trying to bolster Ty's confidence.

Hearing Marcus take charge and provide a solution made Ty feel a whole lot better. Even though he was young, Marcus was proving, time and time again, he was a man in every sense of the word.

Ty called Mya. She needed to make sure nothing happened to her also. Once her mom told her what went down, Mya promised to rush home as soon as possible.

Later that night, Ty and Marcus went out on the hunt. They rode in two separate vehicles. Ty drove her trusty Malibu. Marcus, in a rental. They'd decided to hit up the strip club, *High Rollers!* What other place would allow them to come up with some cash that would equal at least ten thousand dollars?

Marcus waited outside. Ty found a customer going in and persuaded him to accompany her. The club was packed. Based on what she saw, they would definitely be able to hit a nice lick by the end of the night. Even though Ty wasn't a stripper, she had the body of one. Dudes from all over the club were pulling up on her, jocking her drip. One nigga in particular grabbed her arm as she walked by. "Damn, momma. I ain't gon' lie, a nigga trynna go home with you. Fuck these stripper bitches."

Ty feigned irritation. "Boy, you can't afford me," she teased.

Dude frowned his face up. "You think I'm one of these broke niggas?" She could sense he was truly offended. Ty didn't want to run him off.

"Naw, baby boy. I ain't say all that. But, you gotta remember, being broke and being cheap are two different things. You could have all the money in the world, if you ain't willing to take care of a bad bitch, the way she needs to be taken care of, what's the use?" Dude nodded, apparently agreeing with her philosophy.

"What's your name?" he asked, seeing as Ty didn't give a fuck anymore. Her son had been kidnapped. She had less than a year to live. *Fuck it!* She went ahead and told him her real name. "Ty. My name is Ty. And you are?"

"I'm Lil Hitta. And, how much are *you* gonna hit me for?" Ty knew enough to know; she didn't want to low ball herself. She left the ball in his court.

"Well. What do you feel a bitch like me is worth?" she finessed. Since she already shot a slug at his pockets, he thought of an amount high enough, to make it seem as though he had money to blow, but low enough, because he didn't.

"Twenty-five hundred dollars?" Ty made a show, as if she was contemplating the offer. Truthfully, that was way more than she expected him to give her. Plus, the amount was just a prelude. She felt if he had twenty-five hundred dollars to spend on some pussy, he would have at least twice that amount on his person.

Ty tested out her theory. "Do you have a couple dollars, so a girl could get herself a drink?" Lil Hitta reached inside his pocket and pulled out a hefty sized knot. With a quick estimate, Ty believed it to be close to ten bands. *Easy!*

He peeled off a hundred-dollar bill and told her to open up a tab. She grabbed one drink and pocketed the eighty-dollar change. Now that she had her mark, she didn't plan on staying anyway. Ty excused herself and went into the restroom. She texted Marcus. Gave him the scoop on the fish she had on the line. He assured her, he'd be waiting at the rendezvous spot.

Minutes later, with a grab of his dick and a kiss on the neck, Ty persuaded Lil Hitta to leave the club. She hopped in her car and told him to follow her to the motel. Lil Hitta was eager to.

They turned out of the club parking lot. Ty took them down a side street that led to the freeway. The street was a two-lane road, with little to no traffic. She saw an oncoming pair of headlights and slowed her car down, almost to a crawl. The oncoming car passed her up, but stopped directly next to Lil Hitta's Buick Lesabre. *Bocka! Bocka! Bocka! Bocka!*

Shots rang out. Glass shattered. The sound of someone laying on a car horn filled the air. Marcus hopped out of the rental and approached Lil Hitta's driver side window. *'Bocka! Bocka!'* Two more shots pushed his brains into the passenger seat. Marcus opened the door, searched his pockets and relieved Lil Hitta of his money and jewelry.

Then, Marcus hopped back in, just as Ty was pulling off, merging back onto the freeway. Ty headed in one direction. Marcus, in the other. Didn't matter what route they took; both were headed to the same destination. *Home!*

When they got back home, Mya was asleep. Ty counted the money. *Eight thousand, eight hundred and sixty dollars!* Plus the jewelry. They definitely reached their quota for the day. She gave it to Marcus. He placed it with the ninety bands he had stashed.

As he came back downstairs, Ty sat at the dining room table, with a faraway look on her face. He knew she was thinking about CJ. He walked behind her and began to massage her shoulders. Her body instantly began to respond to his touch. Her shoulders slumped. Her breathing became ragged. She purred and moaned as his young but powerful hands did their magic.

Suddenly, Ty grabbed Marcus's right hand, stood up and led him into her bedroom. She felt Mya was old enough to understand her relationship with Marcus. It was always CJ she worried about finding out and being confused.

When she first started sexing Marcus, he was raw energy she had to mold. He definitely had the right equipment. Due to his age, his God-given stamina allowed him to become a certified cocksmith. Right now, that's what she needed.

Ty didn't want love. She wanted to be fucked into oblivion. She needed her pussy to hurt so good that her heart and soul would be left jealous of the pain. As soon as they entered the room, Ty aggressively pulled at his belt. Before his pants could hit the ground, she had her hand in his boxers and his dick out.

Marcus tilted his head back and groaned, as Ty sucked his cock with ferocity. Feeding off of her energy, he knew exactly what she needed. After stepping out of his pants, he grabbed her by her hair. Forcing her on her feet. "Turn around," he growled. She obeyed.

He pushed her forward, ripped her panties clean off, before smacking her on her ass cheeks. The ass cheeks each became warm and turned bright red. Her slit became slick. Marcus grabbed his heavy dick and lined himself up. With one hard push, he buried himself to the hilt. "Agggghh, fuuuucckkk!" Ty screamed, as the young nigga put the dick on her.

Her pussy snapped at his cock. He continued to saw into her. Her brownish, pink booty hole winked his way. He knew that would be the next stop on his tour. "Oh my gawd! Oh my gawd! I'm finna cummmm. I'm cumming. I'm cumming. I'm cummmmiiinnggg." Ty screamed. Marcus showed her no mercy. He knew what her body needed. He would make sure he gave her every inch of it. They fucked each other until total exhaustion took its toll. Neither of them could move a muscle. If only they knew they'd had an audience.

Once she couldn't hear the skin slapping or the wet squelching sounds anymore, Mya removed her ear from her momma's bedroom door and staggered her way back up to her room.

The next evening, the dynamic duo was back on the prowl. Ty led, while Marcus followed. Two cars behind. Each one searching, scheming for some type of opportunity to present itself. Ty spotted an older white woman at the light. She was sitting idly in a crème colored CLK Benz. Something told Ty to keep a tail on her, so she did.

She texted Marcus to let him know what she was on. Ty followed the woman for twenty minutes straight. Finally, they arrived at a bank's drive-through. Ty sat back and watched as the woman took out a substantial withdrawal. An idea beamed into her head. She called Marcus and devised a plan.

For the next half hour, she followed the woman everywhere. First, they went to the coffee shop. Then finally, they made their way to a high rise parking garage. Even though it was risky as hell, Ty followed the woman in. Marcus trailed right behind her. It seemed the old white woman was oblivious to their presence. Trapped in her own world of peace, tranquility and security.

They all continued upwards, until they reached the top floor. The white woman parked first. Then Ty. Marcus parked further down. Ty hurriedly hopped out of her vehicle and made her way to the only entrance to the hallway.

Once there, she feigned as if she lost her key card, rummaging through her purse. The white woman slowly and timidly approached. But, only mildly suspicious. More so irritated than anything else. Ty saw her approach and went into her spiel. "Oh, thank you, Jesus! I seem to have lost my key card," she claimed.

The white woman took a look at Ty and immediately judged her as unfit to have residence in that type of building. So, instead of just using her key card to allow her entry, she asked, "Do you want me to call Joe, so he can let you in?"

Ty didn't know who Joe was. Hell, she didn't even know if there was a Joe. It might've been a trick question, to see if she really resided there. She decided to play it safe. "Uhh. I just moved in last week. I'm not sure who Joe is," she said.

"Oh, Joe is the concierge. He's in charge of assigning the key cards, once they are reported lost or stolen. The white woman began to dig in her purse to retrieve her phone. "I'll just give him a ring. Let him know, you'll be waiting for him on the penthouse floor."

As the woman unlocked her phone, a figure stepped out of the shadows, with animalistic speed. *WHAP!* Marcus decked her with a powerful right cross from behind. The blow landed right above her cheek bone, but below the temple. He felt the hinges on her jaw snap, and break apart. The woman tumbled head first into a parked car and went to sleep.

Ty hurriedly grabbed the whole purse. She knew she didn't have time to go through it on the spot. By the time she ran back and made it safely inside the car, Marcus was already driving his, making his way back down to the ground level. She didn't waste any time. Before long, she'd caught up with him. She approached the exit gate, but Marcus was stalled out. Apparently, you needed an electronic gate key to exit as well as enter. Good thing Ty had the old woman's keys. As soon as she got within ten feet, the gate opened up. Her and Marcus jumped onto the freeway and hightailed it back to 1960.

Once safely back inside the house, Ty dumped the contents of the purse onto the bed. A white bank envelope flopped out. It looked as thick as a 16 oz. steak. Ty opened it up and counted one hundred and thirty crisp one hundred dollar bills. *Thirteen Thousand Dollars! Yessss!*

With what they made the night before, that was close to twenty-five thousand dollars for two nights. Plus, Marcus still had to get rid of the jewelry. He had someone lined up later that night that was interested in buying it.

The jewelry they'd picked up from Lil Hitta wasn't much. A yellow gold bracelet. A customized, buss down Cartier watch. And a yellow gold Jesus piece. When he approached one of his former foster brothers named Lizard about buying it, he wanted to see some pics. So, Marcus sent them. Lizard offered to pay him five thousand dollars for everything.

Marcus knew he could get more, but really wasn't tripping. Time was running out. If they added what they'd made in the last couple days, with what he already had, they'd be about twenty thousand dollars short. With four more days to go, he felt great about his odds.

He stashed all the money inside a shoebox in his closet. He knew that was a primitive spot, but he didn't even want to spend the money to buy a safe. Every dollar counted.

They contemplated going back out, but decided not to push their luck. They didn't want to risk another play, then something terribly wrong occurred. It was always easier to be greedy than to be prudent. Feeling good about the way things were going, they twisted a blunt, got high and made love for the rest of the night.

Chapter 2

Bo woke up, fixed himself a shot of coffee, brushed his teeth, and washed his face. Rose was at work in the laundry and wouldn't be back until after the last chow. So, he had the cell to himself. He stretched and got ready to work out.

He had chest and arms scheduled for that day. After an hour-long workout, he jumped in the bird bath and washed up real good. Then, he got ready to hit the day room. "Commissary. Three row! Commissary!" One of the inmates on one row was alerting the rest of the block, there was a female headed up to their row.

Bo grabbed the smell-good, and hit it a few times. He placed his mirror on the bars. A thick, yellow boned woman was coming down the run. She was about 5"11, maybe six foot even. She had to be one hundred and eighty to one hundred and ninety pounds. With her height, she looked like she was about a hundred and fifty pounds. Her ass was like two NBA basketballs. Bo had heard about her, but this was the first time he laid eyes on her. They said her name was Ms. Cooper.

She'd just gotten off OJT (On the Job Training). This was her first time working in his block. Ms. Cooper was definitely Bo's speed. She wore her pants extra tight. You could clearly see her pussy lips. No doubt, every nigga on the block wanted to fuck that.

Bo watched her sashay down the run. Periodically, stopping in front of cells, to hold conversations with certain inmates. He saw her stop at the cell of a known "jacker" named West God.

West God didn't give a damn. Only cases he caught were code twenty (Masturbation). If you wanted to know if a female faded, or liked to watch that dick, ask West God. Bo watched her walk by his cell and do a double take. Then, she posted up, standing there, talking to him.

Bo could tell by the way she bit her lip, West God was "popping that cock". Two minutes later, she continued down the run. Bo wasn't an advocate for the jack game. That was something he just couldn't get into. He sat on the bottom bunk and acted as if he was reading an urban novel called *Guns Down, Bottoms Up.*

Ms. Cooper saw the book and stopped. "Oh, boy. That's my favorite author," she blurted out.

Bo looked up. "Mines too. I got all his books."

"Oh yeah? That's wassup. You know he's locked up too. He's serving a sixty-seven-year sentence right now," she informed him.

"I didn't know that," Bo admitted. Hearing his favorite author had a bunch of time and was doing something productive with his life made him feel some type of way. Maybe, having all this time doesn't mean your life is over.

"How much time you got?" Ms. Cooper asked him.

"Too much," he replied. She nodded in understanding. "For a murder I didn't do," he added before she even asked.

She studied him for a minute, as if she was trying to decide something. "What do they call you?" she asked.

"Bo."

"Well, Bo, see you around. Good luck with your situation," she told him, as she continued her way down the run. *Damn, she's bad,* he thought. Her perfume lingered in the air. His heart was still beating wildly. That was the first time he'd had a one-on-one with a female of her caliber, since he'd left the world.

As soon as they called an "out", Bo made his way to the day room. Even though he and Cooper were giving each other some serious eye contact, he refused to approach her in public. He liked to be discreet, and felt like niggas who approached women so everybody could see were cornballs.

Bo went back to the cell, right before she did her last security check. She peeped the play. She was anxious to pull up on him, and see what type of timing he was on.

They talked for about ten minutes. Bo noticed she kept staring at his dick print. He knew she was a high-powered freak, and that's just how he liked them.

His dick began to rise. It was something about her that made him want to pull out and start jacking his dick. He didn't want to fuck up his chances though. Some women would let you jack on them, but once you pull your dick out, you throw away any chance of having a meaningful relationship. When she left from in front of his cell, it seemed as if she was slightly disappointed. Bo wondered, is the key to *her* heart through her pussy?

As Cooper walked off the block, Rose was walking onto it. Fresh from work, he didn't want to do much but go in the cell and relax. Knowing he would be hungry, Bo whipped up a taco bowl and had it waiting on him when he stepped in the cell. "Damn. These stupid ass bitches got me all the way fucked up," Rose ranted, as he stomped into the cell. Clearly aggravated.

Bo was still riding high off the encounter he had with sexy Ms. Cooper. Rose was dragging him back down to earth. "What happened?" he asked, only half interested. As Rose went on and explained his day, Bo daydreamed about what he would do the next time he saw Ms. Cooper.

He didn't understand how he'd found himself shacked up with a homosexual. In the world, he never had any gay thoughts. But, since he'd been locked up, it seemed like the only people who were willing to do for him were gay. Now, he was basically married to one.

Bo began to feel ashamed of himself. He had a daughter and a son. How could he explain *this* to them? Would they understand and still love him? "Bo? Bo! You're not even listening." Bo snapped out of his reverie.

"Huh? Look, I'm 'bout to go to the dayroom. I'll be back at rack time," Bo told him. He desperately needed to get some air. Being in the cell with Rose was suffocating him. He wondered, should he try and get moved? Now that there was a "real" woman who was maybe interested in him, he didn't want his living arrangement to fuck that up. Bo spent the rest of the day in the dayroom putting his game plan together.

Bo hadn't seen Cooper on the block in a few days. When she did return, he thought for sure, she'd pull up to his cell. Instead, she walked by without even looking. *What the fuck? Maybe her mind was preoccupied.*

He watched her walk to the end of the run, turn around and head back to the front. She spoke to several different inmates. Bo thought for sure, when she walked by his cell this time, she would speak. Cooper kept her face forward. Once again, walking by without so much as a glance or a peep.

Now, he knew something was up. His mind started racing. Trying to figure out, why the sudden change? Bo checked the clock. He had about another hour before she did her next security check. He sat back and waited. He honestly didn't know what he would say to her. He heard the familiar "three row" call. His mirror came out.

Sure enough, she was coming down the run. She stopped at West God's cell. As usual. When she approached Bo's cell, he spoke up. "Damn, Ms. Cooper. It's like that? You fucked up with a nigga or something?"

At first, it seemed as if she was about to ignore him. Out of respect, she stopped. Her jaw was tight. Her eyebrows furrowed. "Why would you even try and get at me if you know you're gay?"

Bo's heart dropped. "What? What are you talkin 'bout?" He definitely wasn't expecting that. Bo had hoped to remove himself from the situation before it got that far.

"I'm hearing you and your celly fuck around with each other," she spat.

"Who told you that shit?" Bo was beyond pissed. In prison, it seemed, nigga's *stopped* minding their own business. That used to be law. Not anymore. Cooper put her head down.

"I'm not trying to get into all that. I just . . . Really, it ain't even my business. But, I thought maybe you could have been a cool nigga to kick it with . . ."

"Look. On my kids, I'm not gonna say you said shit. Nigga's just hating on a nigga. My celly's a punk, but we don't fuck around with each other. Whoever told you that is on some messy ass, bitch shit. I'm not gonna be able to let it go, so please . . ." Cooper looked like she was giving in, so Bo put the icing on the cake. "If it was you, you'd want to know who it was that was salting your name down."

That seemed to have struck the right nerve. "Do you know a nigga on I Block named Russell? I think y'all call him G." Bo knew exactly who she was talking about. The nigga had been sneak dissing and dropping salt, ever since Bo had pulled up. Every time he confronted dude, G would back down and say he didn't say what they said he said.

Now, he had bit off more than he could chew. Cooper could see that the news really troubled Bo. She was starting to feel as though the rumors weren't true. "He asked me what my favorite block to work was. I told him this block. He asked why. I said, because y'all are laid back. Then, he said, y'all's block was the gay block. I asked him what he meant. He went on to say how y'all had cells where niggas were shacked up, like husband and wife. Then, he took it upon himself to start naming couples. When he said your name, I couldn't believe it."

Bo's eyes began to twitch. His blood boiled. "I appreciate it, Ms. Cooper." He was so mad, he couldn't trust himself to say anything more. Cooper nodded, and kept walking. Bo couldn't wait until the "in and out".

He went ahead and packed up all his shit. He threw on his rec. shoes and plugged in his homemade mouthpiece. Soon as the doors rolled, he shot up out the cell and down the hallway. He made it to I Block's door, and waited anxiously for the CO to open it up.

As he walked on the block, he caught a glance at Cooper staring at him from across the picket. Bo saw one of his potnas, KT, in the day room. "Say, KT, where that nigga G at?"

"He's in the cell. Nigga, what you doing over here? You don't ever fall out of place."

Bo deflected the question. "What cell is the nigga in?"

KT looked at him wearily. "He's in 3-0-6."

Bo ran up the stairs. As soon as he pulled up on G's cell, he went off. G looked like he was listening to some music on his tablet. "Say, bitch nigga, I'm trynna do some punching. Bring your hoe ass out here next in and out, or Imma come up in that bitch," Bo spat.

G was shocked to see him at first, but quickly regained his composure. He played the brave role. "Say, bitch ass, faggot ass nigga. I don't give a fuck about none of that shit. 'Cause you slept that nigga Train, don't mean shit to me." G stood up and now was a few feet away from the bars.

Bo was so hot and angry, yet he couldn't put his hands on him. Instead, he roared back and spat in his face. G wiped the spit off and attempted to spit back, but Bo was already on his way down the stairs.

The "in and out" came. The officer did three-row first. G ran downstairs looking for Bo. He was already in zero-cell,

COUNTDOWN OF A KILLA 2 | LO-LIFE

waiting for him. With no words, as soon as he stepped into the cell, Bo was on him like stink on shit.

His fight with Train wasn't personal. But this . . . Bo was trying to literally beat him to death. No finesse. Just straight gas. G got a couple shots in, but Bo was so amped up, they might as well have been love taps. Bo caught him on the chin with a left hook, then followed it up with a heavy overhand right.

A wide gash opened up above G's left eye. Blood gushed forth like a faucet. Bo hit him hard in his right temple. G staggered. Bo followed up with a heavy left jab, right hook combo. G hit the wall, but was sleep on his feet. Seeing nothing but red, Bo went in for the kill.

By now, twenty different inmates were crowding the run, trying to watch the massacre. Of course, this brought the officers' attention. An ICS was called. Every officer that wasn't tied to a duty post responded.

Bo was sprayed with chemical agents and placed in hand restraints. G was an unconscious, bloody mess. The free world paramedics were called in. When they wheeled G out on the stretcher, it looked as if he'd gotten beat with a weapon. Bo was escorted through the hallway. He was heard screaming out, "Keep my name out y'all mouth. Keep my name out y'all fucking mouths." That served as a warning to the next person that felt like speaking on Bo's name.

As they brought him down to medical, he spotted a wide-eyed Rose at the backdoor to the laundry department. Next to him was Double R. If Bo didn't know any better, they looked guilty of something.

He spent the night in lockup with none of his property. Now that his adrenaline had abated, his hands hurt. Muscles were stiff. He was kicking himself in the ass. *I just beat a nigga's ass, half to death, for telling the truth!*

Real niggas can't be exposed. How can he be upset with a nigga for telling the truth? Now, he was about to be on restricted housing. He wouldn't be able to use the phone for at least forty-five to sixty days. And right now, he needs to communicate, more than ever.

Three days later, Bo laid in his bunk. Someone called his name. "Bo! Look out, Bo!"

"Ayyeee. Who's that?" Bo answered back. Happy to hear someone's voice calling out to him.

"This KT. What cell you in?"

"I'm in sixty-four. Where you at?"

"I'm in sixty-two. What's good?"

"Nigga, what the fuck did you do?" Bo asked.

"Man. Let me tell you. One morning, one of G's lil Blood homies was fucked up because I was screaming for you to max the nigga out. We fucked around and went a couple rounds. We made it the first two times. The third, we got caught. Sgt. Newton saw us in the window. He say he gone write it up like a horse playing case, though. So, they *should* remain a nigga," KT said, hopeful. "What they say they gon' do to you?"

Bo laughed. "G-5 for shit sho. OIG pulled up, talking 'bout the nigga might press charges. Really, I don't give a fuck. Whatever they try to give me, I won't see it until I'm sixty plus. Fuck um!"

"I ain't gon' lie. You beat that niggas ass. *Whatever* he did, bet he won't do *that* no more

"Yeah. Well, hopefully, a nigga won't have to buss up one of his homeboys when I get to G-5. Since I'm solo, you already know they gon' try and push up on me," Bo reasoned.

"Say, look out, Bo. You know I fuck with you the long way. What you do with your dick is your bidness, but I hope you ain't whoop that nigga behind Rose, 'cause . . ." KT left the rest unsaid.

Bo's ears perked up. "Wassup, my nigga?

"Rose fell out of place to Double R's cell yesterday. Look, I ain't want to say shit, because that's your bidness, but that nigga done fucked with all type of niggas on this hoe. He probably felt like you were gonna be in G-5 for a year, so he's letting his hair down.

Bo was honestly hurt. He didn't know what he felt for Rose, but at that very moment, he felt betrayed. He hadn't been gone seventy-two hours and Rose was already sliding in another nigga's cell. "Man, fuck that hoe. I was just playing that role to eat off that bitch," Bo claimed.

"Ohhh yeah? I talked to Ms. Cooper too. She asked me what happened on the block. I told her, a nigga got his ass beat to death. She asked, did I know what for? I told her I didn't know exactly, but I had a feeling. Long story short, she was glad you put that work in," KT reported. That made Bo feel better, but not by much. Even though he was back in her good graces, he couldn't get at her for at least six months to a year. Ain't no telling, she may be gone by the time he makes it back to population.

Bo and KT talked all through the night. The next day, Bo went to court and got slammed. S3 to line 1. Sixty days' restriction, all the way across the board. The day after that, he went to U.C.C. and had gotten G-5'd (closed custody).

As they transferred him to B Block, Bo thought about his kids. So far, he'd made his journey without them. He didn't know how long he could sustain that will power. Bo felt himself cracking under the emotional strain.

His move slip said 2-26T. As he walked down the run, he heard different dudes' conversations. *"Say, Blood, that's that nigga right there...Yeah, they say he hit the homie with a fan motor...Naw, it was shitter brush...What cell is he going to? Who's his celly?"* Bo kept his head up and his mug on, as he made his way to the back of the run. He just hoped his celly was someone he could live with. Either way, he was prepared to go in savage mode if need be.

Chapter 3

Marcus parked Ty's car downtown. All day parking. It'd been a couple weeks since he came to visit his best friend, Chief. A little over six months ago, Marcus and Chief burglarized Chief's sister's boyfriend, Keon's spot.

The two of them hit for fifty pounds of grade-A weed and a couple guns. Because of that, Keon put his hands on Chief's sister, Cindy, even though he really didn't know exactly *who* had robbed him. Of course, Chief and Marcus retaliated. And big bad Keon told the authorities.

Although the boys were masked up, Keon recognized Chief's special edition tennis shoes. Since Chief had been gone, Marcus made sure he put money on his books and sent plenty of pictures. Now, he waited to go see him. At the rate Marcus was going, he didn't know how long he would last on the streets.

Marcus sat in the visitation booth, and waited for Chief to appear. When he finally did, it was all smiles. Chief had gained at least twenty pounds, all muscle. His caramel complexion and spinning waves could easily mistake him for a pretty boy

Before he went to jail, Chief was always the instigator when it came to the two of them getting active. But now, little did he know, Marcus had turned into a full grown savage in his absence.

"Wassup, bro? I see you done got your weight all the way up," Marcus pointed out.

Chief beamed with pride. "Yeah. A nigga been going hard, pushing that floor. Them lil hoes in here be body jocking, so I gotta stay right."

"I can dig that. What they talking bout with your case?" Marcus needed to see his nigga home before anything happened to him.

"Shit. The same shit. That fuck nigga Keon, ratting, as usual. Without him, they ain't got shit. You still don't know where he's at?" Marcus had been hunting Keon down. The word on the street was that he'd skipped town right after Chief went to jail.

"That's why I needed to come see you." With a sly smile, Marcus gave him the good news. "KP said he came back to the city for a family reunion."

Chief's eyes sparkled. "So . . . What's good?"

"I wanted to make sure you still wanted that meal," Marcus told him.

"For shit sho. I know they gon' be looking at me, but fuck it. I'm in jail. That's the best alibi in the world."

"Consider it done then." Chief nodded and the matter was closed.

"Oh yeah. Say, bro, I need you to go check on my T Lady for me. She said you really ain't been by. You know, she looks at you like a son," Chief told Marcus.

Marcus felt a pang of discomfort. He had nothing against Chief's momma, but he really wasn't trying to go see Laura.

"A'ight, dawg. Imma head over there today," Marcus assured him.

"Bet. Tell her I need some of that money she got too." They both began to laugh.

Laura had gotten into a car wreck with an eighteen-wheeler, over a year ago. Even though she wasn't really injured, they settled out of court. After she paid all her fees, she was left with twenty-five thousand dollars. "I got you, my nigga. Hold your head, you'll be home soon. Big facts!" Marcus promised, as he got up to leave.

On his way to Laura's house, he couldn't help but think back to the last time he was over there. It was a night filled with hot, passionate sex. *That* was the reason he'd been avoiding her. His love and loyalty for Chief had him feeling fucked up about fucking his momma.

Marcus pulled up to Laura's house and parked. He didn't know if she had a guest or not. He hoped she didn't. Marcus didn't trust himself being alone with her. By right, Laura was one of the baddest women he knew in person. Not only was she built like a video vixen, but she had her shit together. She'd been raising Chief and Cindy by herself for some time now. She made it all look so easy.

He hopped out and approached the door. He rang the bell and waited. Even though it'd only been a couple months, it felt like years since he'd been there. "Who is it?" a sweet and sultry voice asked from behind the door.

"Marcus."

The door swung open. Laura greeted him with a megawatt smile. "Look what the *cougar* done dragged in," she purred. Marcus took note of her, from top to bottom.

She had on some red satin booty shorts and a matching negligée top. Her nipples were poking out. She looked as if she was getting ready for bed. *This early?*

Marcus's dick began to stir. Laura took her time, hungrily eyeing him also. With a bite of her bottom lip, she stepped to the side. "Come on in, baby." He watched her walk through the house. Hips swaying, ass cheeks jiggling, with each step she took. Her scent was intoxicating. They entered the living room. "Have a seat," she offered. "You want something to drink . . . Or smoke?"

Laura had always been a liberal mom. She would often let Chief smoke and bring girls to the house. He didn't know if it was true, but the rumor was, she had showed Cindy how to put a condom on and give head, by practicing with an 8-inch dildo. "Sure. I can use a drink," Marcus told her.

She fixed them a couple of drinks, then sat them on the coffee table. Laura went into her bedroom and returned with a sack of weed and a cigarillo. "Do you know how to roll?"

Marcus nodded. She tossed him the sack. "Where's Cindy?" he thought to ask.

"Oh, she's at her friend's house, until tonight. So, it's just us for a couple of hours," she slyly said. Marcus had the blunt twisted up in no time. Laura got up to go retrieve some matches. Her satin shorts were stuffed all into her ass crack. The dew from her sex lips had the shorts sticking to her crevices.

His dick was forming a tent in his Ralph Lauren cargo pants. She sat back down directly across from him and lit the blunt. After a few hits, Laura leaned over the coffee table and passed it to him. Marcus hit it twice, then told her the reason for his visit. "I went to see Chief. He told me to come by and check on you. Plus, he said to tell you to get that money up outta there." The last part was said with a smile.

As he passed the blunt back to Laura, her manicured nails grazed over his hand. Chills ran through his body. She giggled, then smirked. "Is *that* all you came here for?" she asked him seductively.

Marcus took in a deep breath. "Look, Ms. Sage—"

"Boy, what I tell you about that Ms. Sage business! We're way past formalities. Wouldn't you say?"

Marcus rubbed his head nervously. "Yeah, I guess you're right. Okay then. Every time I get around you, you do something to me. Something I can't explain or seem to control. And . . . I just don't wanna do my nigga like that."

She waited for Marcus to conclude before she took one more sip, then sat her glass down. With her legs splayed open, Marcus couldn't do much but stare at her camel toe. The front of her satin shorts were damp, a darker shade of red. She caught him looking, reached down and pulled her crotch band to the side. Her meaty sex lips popped out, her clit already swollen and slick with dew.

Marcus subconsciously licked his lips, remembering the taste of her sweet cum when she flooded his mouth. "I love my son, Marcus. But, my son doesn't control *this* right here," she said, as she patted her pussy. "Momma gon' do what she wanna do. That's the difference between a girl and a woman. That's also the difference between a boy and a man. Now, I know you *look* like a man. You've got a grown man's dick. But, do you have the *balls* of a man?" She cocked one leg up onto the coffee table. "Now, come tell momma. Are you a boy or a *man*?"

Blame it on the weed, the liquor, or both. Marcus couldn't take it anymore. He stood up, walked around the coffee table until he was standing directly in front of her.

With a quick tug, Laura pulled his shorts down. Marcus stepped out of them. She peeled his boxers off next. His cock sprang forth like a diving board. Laura gripped his thighs with both hands, then scooped his cock into her mouth. His plum-sized dick head felt great against her tongue. "Hmmmm," she moaned. Laura began to work her neck.

Marcus tucked the helm of his shirt under his chin. That way, he could get a clear and unobstructed view of Laura eating his dick. *Ghlup. Ghlup. Ghlup.* Her cheeks ballooned, in and out. Marcus stroked her mouth like he would her cat.

"I want some of that pussy," he said huskily. She eased back, allowing his dick to flop free. She stood up, shimmied out of her shorts and threw her top onto the floor. Laura turned around, facing the couch and leaned forward.

Her coochie popped out at him. It opened up like a rose petal. She looked back. "Come get it." Marcus removed his shirt. Only thing he had on was his Jordan socks. He grabbed ahold of his dick, lining it up with the mouth of her pussy. The heat from her box snapped at his cock. Her walls hugged him tightly. Like a lost relative.

Marcus slid all his length into her. "Agghhhh," Laura shrieked. The young nigga gave her no respite. He began to rock his hips, bussing her pussy open. Her big ole ass cheeks crashed against his abs. *Clap. Clap. Clap. Clap.* He kept on pounding, holding on to her hips as she reached under and diddled her clit. "Oh shit! Oh shit! I'm cumming . . . Fuucckk, son. Momma's finna cum all over that dick."

Laura's pussy twitched and spasmed. She came, squirting back at him. Her pussy felt like a warm water balloon. Marcus slid back, squatted down and drank, as her cum poured into his mouth. He took the time to inhale her crinkly rosebud. She smelled fresh and clean. He spread her cheeks apart, and licked up and down her crack.

She shivered. Marcus wasn't done just yet. He turned her around and had her sit back on the couch. She cocked her legs up and held them wide apart. He dropped to his knees, grabbed his cock, and slid right back into her dripping, wet gash. Balls deep!

Laura grabbed on her titties, massaging and pinching her nipples. Marcus continued to stroke her insides loose. Her cum bubbled up and ran down the crack of her ass. Her pussy began to queef. Marcus looked down at the joining. Her sex lips pulled at his shaft, as his dick continued to scrape her G-spot. "Damn, boy. I gotta have this dick. You hear me? Shit, momma needs this young cock, baby . . . Cum for me. Cum for momma," she urged.

Marcus felt his balls tighten. His shaft was covered in white, creamy froth. His muscles quivered. "Agggh, fuucckk! I'm finna cum. I'm finna . . ." He thought to pull out, but Laura locked her heels together, pressing down on his ass. She pulled him further into her, as his balls exploded, emptying deep inside her cunt, filling her to the brim. His cum seeped out the corners and the crevices of her coochie.

He pulled out, dick slimy and saturated with cum. Laura sat up and licked him clean. Once he was back fully loaded, she invited him to her round, brown dookie shoot. Marcus spent the rest of the afternoon fucking her so good, that when he left, she wrote him a check for one thousand dollars.

She told him she would put the money on Chief's books. That the band was for him. "It's more where that came from. If I can get more of *this*," she said, while gripping his spent cock. Getting paid made the betrayal a little more bearable.

Still, Marcus didn't want to pull up to the crib he shared with Ty, just yet. Not smelling like another woman. He stopped at a motel, paid for an hour and washed up. When he got back home, Ty was still out and about. Mya was upstairs, talking loudly on her phone. Marcus overheard her telling one of her girlfriends about a guy named Jeremiah.

Little did he know, Jeremiah's uncle—Pat—is the same one he robbed. The same one that was responsible for little CJ coming up missing.

Chapter 4

J Wright sat at the dining room table, weighing up an ounce of crack. He had just gotten done cooking and was eager to get rid of it. He held it up to the light, to make sure it didn't have any "rat holes" in it. After dabbing it with a napkin, he threw it on the scale. *23.8 grams.* He smiled. Considering he only dropped fourteen grams in the pot, to bring back twenty-four, straight butter, he thought to himself, *Not bad.*

He broke it down into dimes and placed them all in a sandwich bag, with the other rocks. Altogether, he had over five hundred dime rocks in a heavy duty, Glad Ziploc bag. J Wright hated the fact he had to pass everything off to the little homies to hustle. *Why?* Because he was on babysitting duty.

A few days ago, he'd escorted some bitch Pat was fucking, to snatch up some little brat. Pat told him he'd pay him ten bands to watch the rugrat for the week. It'd only been a few days, but the shit was driving him crazy.

It wouldn't have been so bad, if he could have left, every now and then. Or, at least bring some bitches over. But, Pat made it very clear. J Wright was not to leave, and one was to come over. Well, except the smoker who stayed there. Carleen.

Carleen was only forty-two years old, but the drugs and the streets made her look much older. She had just done ten years flat in prison, for fraud, as well as aggravated assault.

If you judged her by her body, you would never believe she smoked crack.

She was 5'6", one hundred and fifty-five pounds. Smooth mocha colored skin. Light brown eyes, with a thirty-eight-inch ass. Back in the day, she was hands down one of the baddest chicks in the game.

She started smoking crack when she was nineteen. Her boyfriend at the time was a nigga from 5th Ward, named LeLe. People thought he was a stomped down hustler. Whole time, he was just a glorified dope fiend.

He'd introduced her to smoking premos one night. Not long after, she was a full-blown crack addict. She'd been one of J Wright's most loyal customers for years. Matter of fact, when he first jumped off the porch, selling dope, she was the first one he tricked off his dope to. She gave him a shot of head one night, while his mom was out with her home girls, playing Pitty Pat. That was six years ago.

Since then, she'd shown him how to improve his whip game. Bringing him so much money, she'd have been his Bottom Bitch, if he was pimping.

As he finished in the kitchen, Carleen was watching *Law and Order*. J Wright despised the show. He pulled out his phone, scrolling through his social media page. IG models were posting videos and going live. Popping pussy on camera. *Fuck it!* "Carleen!" he called out.

She turned her head around. "Wassup?"

"Here." J Wright tossed three dime rocks onto the dining room table. Her eyes lit up. She quickly got off the couch and made her way over to him, her beige Capri pants riding up her ass crack. She stopped in front of him, knees locked, standing on her back legs. J Wright had already found the time to pull his dick out. He sat there stroking it. Carleen had serviced him enough times to know what he wanted. He also knew what *she* needed first.

She went into the kitchen, pulled out a straight shooter and sat next to him. She stuffed one of the dimes into the cylinder, then lit it. A thick, gray, pungent smoke filled the air. After the first hit, her eyes sparkled. Her jaw began to twitch.

J Wright could see her juices start to saturate through her panties, dampening the crotch of her capris. Her legs began to open and close, like a butterfly's wings. She sat back, and let the drug do its thing.

Once her high leveled out, she dropped to her knees. Carleen was a hood renowned dick sucker. Especially, when she had that good dope in her system. *Ghlup. Ghlup. Ghlup. Ghlup.* Her neck moved with fluid efficiency, as she gobbled up his cock. She fondled his balls, as he closed his eyes imagining his mom's home girl eating his dick instead of a smoker.

When he finally opened his eyes back up, the little annoying rugrat was just standing there. Looking lost and sad. "What the fuck! Take your lil dirty ass back in the room, before I take my belt off and whoop you," J Wright yelled. Little CJ jumped back. Startled, he ran back into the bedroom scared, eyes full of tears.

The only reason he'd gotten into the car that day was because of Aunt Meme. But, she dropped him off at the mean man's house. They'd given him a bath, but barely any food. The lady was sort of nice to him, but the man was always mean.

CJ couldn't understand why. All he did was stay in his room all day. Only reason he came out that time was to ask for some food. He hadn't eaten since yesterday morning. His stomach was starting to hurt really bad. Every chance he got, he closed his eyes and prayed that Aunt Meme or his momma would come get him.

The school bell rang. All the students rushed out. Except for Mya and Jeremiah. Reason being, they weren't at school. They were at his uncle's duck off spot. The spot they'd spent the last *three* days at, having sex like it was going out of style.

Jeremiah had finally broken up with his girlfriend, Roxy. He and Mya were officially a couple. As they were leaving the apartments, Jeremiah's phone rang. He noticed his uncle Pat's number, and smiled. "Wassup, Uncle Pat?" he answered cheerfully.

"Where you at?"

"I'm just leaving the hideout, about to drop my girlfriend off."

"Okay. I see you, boy. Well, look, can you do me a favor? Can you slide by the pharmacy and pick me up a couple things? Your aunt's spending the weekend with her momma. I ain't got nobody else to grab what I need. Plus, it will give me a chance to meet your girl."

"A'ight, bet. I got you. Jeremiah was happy to be able to do something for his uncle. He turned to Mya. "Do you gotta go home? Like, right now, *right now*?"

"Well, not really. Ever since my lil brother went missing, my mom's been wanting me to come home as soon as school is over with, but . . . Why, wassup?"

"My uncle called. He needs somebody to grab him a few things. He's still banged up, so he can't move around on his own," Jeremiah explained.

Mya shrugged. "Okay." Truth be told, her nose was so wide open, he could have told her they were going on a deep space voyage, and she would have been down to ride. Since they started messing around, Mya had fallen madly in love.

Every waking moment was spent daydreaming about Jeremiah. But, that highway of love was a two-way street. Jeremiah couldn't stop thinking about her either. In his young mind, she was the one. He was eager to bring her to his uncle and get his seal of approval.

After picking up the items, they drove to Pat's two-story brick home in the New Forest subdivision. Even though Pat was knocking on seven figures, he lived rather modestly. He was the type of hustler that was made to last in the game. He might not have made the biggest splash, but when it was said and done, he might get the last laugh.

Jeremiah parked. Both him and Mya made their way to the front door. Pat had already texted him, and told him to *just walk in.* Mya was in awe of how the house was decorated. You could tell it was a home that embodied a woman's touch. They found Pat sitting in the living room with his leg propped up. "Hey, Unc," Jeremiah greeted.

"Wassup, Ju Ju," Pat sang, calling Jeremiah by his family nickname. "Who's this lovely lady?"

"Oh, this is my girlfriend. Mya, meet my uncle Pat. Uncle Pat, meet Mya."

"Nice to meet you, sir," Mya shyly responded.

"Nice to meet you too, young lady." Pat turned to Jeremiah. "Okay. I see you got taste like your good ole Uncle Pat, huh? What y'all 'bout to get into?"

"Well, I'm 'bout to take her home." Pat was about to ask, *where did she stay?* But, his phone rang. He had his thumb on the ignore button, but he saw it was J Wright, so he figured he'd better answer it

Pat answered, then told the caller to "hold on", while he dismissed the pair. "I gotta take this call. Go ahead and take lil momma home, but make sure you swang back by here before you go to the house," Pat told Jeremiah. "Once again, nice to meet you, Mya," Pat called out, before he put the phone back up to his ear.

As they walked out the house, Mya admitted, "Your uncle seems cool as hell."

"Yeah, your Aunt Meme seems cool as hell too. Especially, since she didn't snitch you out about skipping school."

"Oh naw. One thing about my Aunt Meme, she can definitely keep a secret," Mya admitted. Jeremiah threw the truck in drive, and headed back to Humble.

When they pulled up to the house, Ty was outside, waiting on them. Ever since CJ had been abducted, Ty didn't take any chances with Mya. Even though she allowed Mya to ride home with her boyfriend, Ty made her check in, on the regular. "How you doing, ma'am?" Jeremiah called out to Ty.

"Hey, Jeremiah. Thank you for bringing her home." The couple hugged and kissed, before Jeremiah jumped back in the SUV and took off. Ty watched as he drove away. There was something about him that seemed awfully familiar. She shook it off, and followed Mya back into the house.

Jeremiah had made it back to his uncle's house. Now, he and Pat were watching the Rockets play the Mavericks. "I need you to do me a favor," Pat asked his nephew.

"What's good?"

"I need you to take Meme to go see J Wright," Pat said. Jeremiah's face contorted. He didn't understand why he had to pick Meme up when she has her own car.

Pat noticed, and tried to clean it up. "If I tell her to go on her own, she'll figure out some way out of it. She hates J Wright," Pat lied.

That seemed to make sense to Jeremiah. "Okay, Unc. I got you.'"

"I really appreciate that. What's up with you and ole girl?"

Jeremiah's face lit up. "I think I love her. For real, for real."

Pat chuckled. "So, the pussy must be good as hell." Jeremiah blushed. "So?" Pat pushed. "Does she have some good, or what?"

"Yeah," Jeremiah finally admitted.

"That's wassup. But good pussy is only ten percent. You need a girl that's loyal and can think. A lot of these females out here are dumb as a box of rocks. You show them a *lil* money, and they'll cross out the nigga they've been dealing with their entire lives. Make sure she's worth giving your heart to, before you hand it over," Pat schooled. Jeremiah nodded, as he soaked up the top flight game.

After a while, Meme called to say she was ready. Jeremiah hopped in the truck, and took off to go get her. When he pulled up, he saw crackheads walking around. Dudes with bandannas hanging out their back pockets. They were just standing there, looking as if they were waiting for somebody to trip with. Jeremiah really didn't want to get out of the car, but did anyway.

As he walked through the breezeway, a dude who looked to be about his age approached him. "Who you over here to see, my nigga?"

"Uhhh. Meme?" Dude looked at him skeptically. Trying to decipher if Meme was fucking with dudes *his* age.

After a small moment, dude nodded. "A'ight." Then, he walked off. Jeremiah continued, until he reached Meme's door.

Knock! Knock! Knock! She opened up the door, barely dressed. Clad in a black and red set of matching panties and bra. "Jeremiah!" she sang out. "Go ahead and come in." Meme turned around and walked towards the back. He stared at her panty-covered backside. Ass cheeks hanging out. She must've sensed him staring. She looked back over her shoulder and said, "My bad. I had spilled some spaghetti sauce on my clothes. Gotta change. Just have a seat, I'll be right out."

Jeremiah couldn't help but to stare at her ass cheeks, as they jiggled in her laced panties. Meme was hands down a bad bitch! Even though she was his uncle's chick, he wanted to someday get a piece of her. He regretted not taking his uncle up on that offer.

"Sure. Take your time," he told her sheepishly. Jeremiah sat down in her living room and played on his phone until she came out.

COUNTDOWN OF A KILLA 2 | LO-LIFE

"Okay. I'm ready." She'd thrown on a slim, fitting, lavender sundress, with some designer sandals. Her scent had Jeremiah's mouth drooling. She walked past him and left a faint trace of honeysuckle.

He followed her out of the apartment, and into his SUV. The whole time, his eyes were glued to her ass. Meme threw an extra twist in her step, knowing the young nigga was watching. "Do you know where J Wright's trap is?" she asked.

Jeremiah shook his head by way of saying "no". His uncle never exposed him to the streets like that. His whole life, he'd been pampered and groomed to play ball. As long as he played ball, his uncle would get him anything he wanted. "It's not that far. Just get on the freeway and take 610 South. I'll tell you when to exit." Fifteen minutes later, they were pulling up to Carleen's house in South Park. "Just wait here," Meme said, as she hopped out.

Meme walked in and was sick to her stomach. The house smelled rancid. A thick cloud of crack smoke permeated the air. In the living room was Carleen and two of her smoker friends, getting higher than dope prices. "Where's J Wright?" Meme asked. She just wanted to get this over with.

She hated herself for what she was doing. Even though he called her Aunty, CJ was like a son to her, especially since she didn't think she could have any kids. "He's in the restroom," Carleen answered. Her eyes had a glassy sheen to them.

Meme didn't want to wait. She ventured to the back bedroom. She walked in. CJ was laying on the floor, wrapped up in a dirty blanket, his head hidden beneath. He heard someone come in and peeked from underneath his hiding spot.

He saw her. His eyes lit up like two lightbulbs. "Aunt Meme!" He jumped up and almost ran her over, trying to give her a hug. She felt him trembling in her arms. She didn't know if it was from fear or joy. Her heart broke, when she saw the state he was in. Plus, he smelled horrible. Tears threatened to fall down her face.

"Hey, Pooh Bear. You hungry?"

"Aunt Meme. I wanna go home. Pleeaaseee. I don't like it here," he pleaded.

"You will go home soon, sweetie. Your mom had to go out of town. She wanted me to take care of you while she's gone," Meme claimed.

"Why can't I just go to your house then? The man over here is always mean. He keeps yelling at me. Saying bad words."

"Is that why you're hiding underneath your blanket?

"Yeah. But, it's because of the smell too," CJ expressed. Seeing him like this broke her heart in a million pieces. But, she was in too deep. She couldn't turn back now.

"I'll be right back, Pooh Bear," she assured him. She made Jeremiah take her to Wal-Mart. She bought new clothes, soap, a toothbrush, a new blanket and bedsheets. She picked up his favorite pepperoni and pineapple pizza and even bought him a Nintendo DS, so he could be occupied.

When Meme returned, J Wright's was sitting at the kitchen table, weighing up crack. She didn't even bother to acknowledge him. Instead, she simply just brought CJ the pizza, watched him eat until he was full, then put him in the tub and scrubbed him clean. Once he was dry, she sat with him in her arms, rocking back and forth until he was sleeping peacefully. Meme left the room. Heavy-hearted.

As she was leaving out the front door, she looked at J Wright with menace in her eyes. "Look, nigga. That little boy's like a son to me. If I come back and he's in the state he was in, on my soul, Imma fuck you up." Something about the way she said it made J Wright a believer.

Meme slammed the front door behind her. The tears came crashing down. She didn't want Jeremiah to see her like this. She couldn't bear to step foot back in that house, so she stood on the front porch, crying her soul out. Meme cried and cried until she couldn't cry anymore.

Chapter 5

When Meme finally returned to the car, Jeremiah was busy texting someone. For some reason, when he saw Meme, he became self-conscious and tried to hide his phone. She glanced down and saw Mya's name on the screen. "What you 'bout to do, Jeremiah?"

"I guess take you back to your crib."

"Are you in a rush?" Meme asked him.

"Well, do you think you could swing by Mya's momma house. I wanna go spend a little time over there." Even though logic suggested she stayed as far away from the family as possible, Meme felt so bad about the situation, she thought she needed to face them instead. She owed it to them to be there. Plus, her absence would only cause suspicion.

Jeremiah couldn't hide his joy, even if he wanted to. "Sure. I can do that." He happily texted Mya, and told her he was bringing her aunt over.

Mya texted back, with the heart and thumbs up emoji. On the ride over there, Meme analyzed Jeremiah. Even though he had some of the same facial features as Pat, they were nothing alike.

She couldn't picture Jeremiah arranging the kidnapping of a little boy. Then again, who would have ever thought Meme would be a participant in that same kidnapping. A little boy she watched grow up from infancy.

When they finally pulled up, Meme saw that Ty's car was gone. She really wanted a chance to gauge Ty, and see how her collecting of the ransom money was coming along. She prayed the money would be paid, because she didn't know what Pat would do if it wasn't.

Minutes after they arrived, Mya came bouncing out of the house, happier than a pig in slop. "Hey, Auntie," she sang.

"Hey, girl. Where your momma at?"

"Her and Marcus had left, right before y'all texted and said y'all were on the way."

"Did she say what time they would be back?"

Mya knew they would be gone all night, but she feared if she told Meme that, she would want Jeremiah to take her back home. So, Mya *kind of lied.* "Uhmm. She really didn't say but it shouldn't be long."

Meme could see through Mya's bullshit. Still, she decided to play along. "Okay. Well, I don't mind waiting a lil while. If Jeremiah ain't tripping."

They both looked at him expectantly. The look of relief on his face was evident. He was eager to spend some time with Mya, and would have stayed there all night waiting on Ty, if need be. "Oh. I ain't doing no tripping."

"Well. That's settled. Imma go use the little girls' room, I'll be right back." With that, Meme went inside, while the two love birds sat in the truck.

As soon as she stepped into the house, Meme didn't waste any time. She frantically searched the kitchen, Meme's bedroom, and the living room. *Nothing!* Then, she traveled upstairs. She searched Mya's bedroom first. Meme found a dildo and a sack of weed. She shook her head as she tossed them under Mya's bed.

Then, it was onto CJ's room. As soon as she crossed the threshold, she regretted it. All his toys were scattered over the floor. You could tell, someone decided to leave his room just as he left it. His handheld game system still laid in his unmade bed.

Meme picked up his favorite miniature football. She told herself she would bring it to him, next time she went to visit.

She knew it would give him a sense of comfort to see something from home. Meme traveled into the last room.

She was surprised to see how neat and tidy it was. To be eighteen, Marcus was very organized. The room had a state-of-the-art Bose system, fifty-six-inch flat screen, and a king-size bed with red and black Fendi print, comforters and sheets.

Meme searched under the bed first. Then, she moved to the dresser drawers. Last was the closet. He had an assortment of clothes, but nothing too extravagant. It seemed like his bed was the only thing over the top. His shoe collection was modest.

She hurriedly checked the boxes. Her eyes scanned frantically for anything out of place. Then she spotted it. *A duffle bag.* She snatched it, unzipped it and her heart skipped a beat. Her pussy instantly became wet with greed. There, inside the bag, was stacks upon stacks of money. Rubber banded and bundled up.

The ransom money! A large part of her was relieved that they did have it. But, another part of her—the grimy, greedy, demonic part of her—wanted to take the money for herself. With it, she knew she could turn her life all the way around. Maybe, she could put down on a house. Or, start a small business. All types of possibilities floated in her mind.

Then, she thought about CJ. Now that she thought about it, what would Pat *really* do, if Ty didn't come up with the money? He wasn't about to kill a kid. *Was he?* No, of course not, she rationalized. The problem she was now facing was: how she was going to get out of the house with the money. Meme sat back and thought about it. Then, it hit her. *The window!*

She opened it up and looked out. The view was of the backyard. Her mind began to race. She picked up the bag and tossed it out the window. It landed in the grass with a loud "thud". As an afterthought, she scooped up the nerf football and tossed that out the window. Meme, then made her way down the stairs, and out the front door.

As Meme approached the SUV, Jeremiah and Mya were locked in a very passionate embrace. "Uggh-Um." She cleared her throat. Both of them jumped, startled as they broke apart. "I hate to break this up, but something's come up and I have to get to the house. Matter of fact, y'all two need to get ready for school in the morning, anyway. Mya. Tell your momma, I'll catch up with her later."

"Okay, Aunty." Mya focused her attention back on Jeremiah. "Bye, baby. See you tomorrow," she said, as she made her way back to the house.

Meme could smell a faint scent of pussy. Every time Jeremiah would move his hand, she would get a whiff of it. The ride back to the house was so nerve wracking, Meme couldn't do much, but sit there and think. *Was she making the right decision? What will Pat do about CJ, if they don't pay?* All these questions flooded her mind, as her and Jeremiah rode in silence.

After he dropped her off, she made it seem as if she was headed inside. Instead, as soon as she knew the coast was clear, she double backed and jumped in her car.

Meme hightailed it back to Ty's house. She parked down the streets and walked the rest of the way. Her palms sweated. Her heart thundered. She prayed Ty and Marcus didn't pull up, just as she was walking off with the bag, red-handed.

She approached the driveway and exhaled. A great big sigh of relief. The coast was clear. *For the moment.* She ran across the driveway, to the side of the house.

Meme crept into the backyard. There was a tiny part of her that hoped Mya came out and found the bag, thus preventing her from the moral dilemma she was forcing herself into. *No!* The bag was still there.

She snatched the bag up, turned and ran out the backyard. Once she made it down the street, she slowed to a walk.

Meme hopped into the car and just sat there, gripping tightly onto the steering wheel. Huge gulps of air filled her lungs, her heart working overtime. Sweat poured down her face, stinging her eyes. She steadied her nerves, cranked the car up, then headed home.

Meme knew, once Ty and Marcus found out what happened, they would come knocking. She immediately bought a storage space and locked the duffle bag in there. Until she could find a better hiding spot, that would have to do.

When she walked into the apartment, Slick was in his usual spot. Getting high and playing video games. Maybe it was her new found fortune, but Meme was finally fed up.

After a heated discussion, she asked Slick to leave. And, as always, he refused. Thinking Meme would eventually calm down. This time, she had a trick for his ass.

While he was sitting down, she walked up and punched him as hard as she could in the side of the head. Slick slunk back, looking at her as if she'd lost her mind. Once he recovered from the initial shock, he got dead on her ass.

Meme covered up her face, allowing a few body blows, before sprinting into her room, locking the door and calling the cops. "Hello. Yes, can you please send someone to my house. My boyfriend's been beating on me and I think he's trynna to kill me," she cried.

Meanwhile, Slick was oblivious. He went right back to playing video games and smoking a blunt to calm his nerves.

Fifteen minutes later, and much to his dismay, the cops were at the door. As soon as Meme heard the door knocking, she came out of the room, her best Oscar winning performance on display. Slick was hauled away for Assault/Family Violence.

To be honest, Meme didn't give two fucks about Slick going to jail. She needed a break, and if he wasn't willing to walk away, she would have him carried away. In cuffs!

Once he was gone, she cleaned up after him. Then, she hopped inside the shower and fantasized about what she would spend the money on. This, by far, was the most money she'd ever had. Before she put it in storage, she counted it. *One hundred and forty-one thousand two hundred eighty-two dollars!*

Knowing she had that much money made her pussy wet. She needed to celebrate. After getting out of the shower and applying her smell-good, she pulled out her phone and scrolled through the contacts. She smiled when she saw a familiar face. *Andrew.*

Andrew, or Drew, as everyone in the apartment complex called him, was a twenty-three-year old D-Boy, who was on the rise. At six foot, weighing two hundred and ten pounds, with brown eyes and a milk chocolate skin tone, he had his share of women. His baby momma, Kat, was a jealous woman, who didn't mind fighting over her man. And it just so happened that her and Meme were cool. *Or so she thought.* Meme texted him.

Meme: *?#? (That was the code. If he had possession of his phone, he would know how to reply). It took a few minutes for him to answer back.*

Drew: *#!#*

Meme: *What u doing?*

Drew: *Chilling. Watching the game.*

Meme: *Hungry? (smiley face emoji)*

Drew: *Y...U gone feed me.*

Meme: *U know I will. Hurry up.*

Drew: *OTW*

Four minutes later, he was at her door. Rocking sweats and a black wife beater. Meme had on a short, pink satin robe, which was tied at the waist. Nothing underneath, but baby oil. No words.

She led him to the same couch her nigga was just sitting on an hour ago. Meme sat on the couch and had him stand between her opened legs. She pulled his sweats down. He stepped out of them. Next, she peeled his boxers off. His eight-inch dick flopped out and hung in front of her like a ripe banana. She inhaled his scent, then pulled the skin back on his uncircumcised cock. With one gulp, Meme had half his dick stuffed down her throat. She bobbed her head until he became hard as an iron pipe.

She pulled him out and began to rub his meat all over her face, leaving a small trace of saliva and precum in its wake. Meme didn't think she could ever be faithful. She loved dick too much. Sometimes, she'd be so horny, she would have sex with three different niggas in one day. Morning, noon and night.

Meme ducked her head under Drew's dick, scooping his balls into her mouth. She rolled them around, loving the taste of skin on her tongue. Drew moaned, while grabbing the sides of her head. "Let me get some of that pussy, baby," he whispered.

She leaned back and cocked her legs in the air. Her sex lips glistened, as she slid her right middle finger up and down her slit. Drew dropped to his knees. He snatched her forward. Her ass hung off the edge of the couch cushion.

He watched her juices drip down and disappear in the valley between her fluffy ass cheeks. Drew lined himself up. Meme reached for him, guiding him home. "Sssshittt!" she hissed, as he filled her up.

Drew grabbed her by the neck, squeezed, and began to work his hips. Meme's pussy pulled at him, squeezing, choking his cock with each stroke. She grabbed the back of her thighs, and opened herself up even wider.

He used his left hand to diddle her clit, his right hand gripping her neck. She leaked all over his rod. Before she could cum, he pulled out and made her turn around.

With her knees on the carpet, her face stuffed between the couch cushion, Drew slapped her on her ass cheeks, before slamming his dick back into her hot box.

Meme's ass wobbled, as it crashed back into his abs, heating up Drew's midsection. "Ooh shit! Fuck, baby. That dick feels sooo good," she cried out, as he punished her guts. He stuck his right thumb in her mouth, wet it, then plugged her tight, little ass hole with it.

She started going crazy. Thoughts of getting double-penetrated began to creep into her mind. A tidal wave came crashing down. "Awww, fuck. I'm finna cum. Oh my gawd . . . I'm cummminnmngg!"

With her fist clenched, her face stuffed into the couch cushion, Meme shook, then spewed nut all over Drew's thick ass dick. Her booty hole began to pulsate around his thumb. He pulled it out and watched her asshole wink at him.

He slipped out of her snatch, and worked the crown of his cock through her anal ring. Meme flinched. "Ssshhh . . . Take this dick like the slut you are, Meme. Ain't you a nasty little slut?" He taunted as he broke through her barrier, his whole head buried inside her rectum.

"Uh. Uh. Yessss. I'm a slut!" she howled. Drew pushed a few more inches in. Meme's anal walls collapsed around his cock, locked on like a python. He looked down, and the sight of seeing his dick sticking out the hole in her ass did something to him. It was like a flag pole, stuck into the ground. *Marking his territory.*

He reared back and began to saw into her bowels. She screamed. Panted. Pounded the couch cushion, as Drew fucked her asshole to shreds. "Agh. Aghhh. I'm 'bout to nut. Fuck, Meme. I'm cumming." He planned on pulling out, but her booty hole was so warm and inviting, he couldn't. His dick threw up all in her dookie shoot.

Meme felt him fill her up. Another orgasm wrecked her body. When Drew finally did pull out, rivulets of cum poured forth, leaking down the backs of her thighs.

They spent the rest of the night fucking each other's brains out. Meanwhile, Slick was blowing up her cell phone. Calling from the County Jail.

Ty and Marcus were headed home. All in all, it was a decent night. After robbing a dice game, Marcus came away with fourteen bands. With the hundred and forty thousand dollars they had at the house, they'd finally met their goal. With two days to spare, Ty couldn't contain her excitement. She stared at Marcus as he drove. Her feelings for him grew deeper with each passing day. She watched him grow from a boy to a man. Not just any man, but the type of man she needed and desired. A man that would stand on business. Loyal. Devoted. A go-getter!

Never would she have thought she could leave Bo for anybody else. Now, she was actually feeling as though she could. Marcus checked all of her boxes. Not to mention, his dick was "oh so good". And his head had her climbing up the walls. What he lacked in experience, he made up for in exuberance. She had it on her mind to unleash the freak when they got home. Ty planned on showing him things only a husband should see.

When they got back to the house, they immediately noticed the back yard gate was wide open. Neither one of them remembered going into the back yard. Matter of fact, since CJ had been kidnapped, they hadn't been anywhere but to and from the car. It could have only been one person. *Mya!* They both thought.

As they stepped inside, Marcus immediately made his way upstairs to stash away the money. As soon as he stepped foot in his bedroom, he knew something was wrong. He made a silent prayer, hoping he was just tripping. As he inched closer and closer to his closet, he knew what he would find.

Sure enough, he opened the closet door and immediately noticed the duffle bag was missing. He ran out of the room and barged into Mya's room without knocking. The room had a pleasant smell of fresh pussy. She had the phone to her ear, her eyes closed, her fingers digging up in her coochie.

She whispered Jeremiah's name, so Marcus assumed she was having phone sex. He hated to disturb her privacy, but the matter was of utmost importance. "Mya!"

Mya jumped, snatched the blanket over her privates. "What are you doing?" she shrieked.

"I apologize, but I need to talk to you. Can you please get dressed?" Marcus averted his eyes, but his brain was already stained.

"Okay. Okay. Just please . . . Get out of my room," she stammered, embarrassed. Marcus felt bad about causing her to expose herself like that to him. He went downstairs and waited for her to come down.

Ty could tell something was wrong. "Bae. What's the matter?"

"The money! It's missing."

Ty's eyes grew big as saucers. "What? What you mean it's missing? No, no, no. Please don't say that shit. Mya! Mya!" Ty became frantic, desperate for answers.

"I told her to come downstairs, but I haven't said anything about the money missing yet. She's getting dressed right now," Marcus assured her.

Sure enough, seconds later, Mya came downstairs in some shorts and one of Jeremiah's old football jerseys. She saw the look on their faces and knew she had royally fucked up, somehow.

Before she could ask what's wrong. "Did you have someone in the house?" Ty wasted no time in grilling her.

At first, Mya didn't even consider Meme. "No. Why?"

"The money is missing. So bitch, you better not be lying," Ty seethed.

Mya looked confused. "Wait. What money?" Ty had purposely neglected to tell Mya that the people that had CJ wanted a ransom. She didn't want Mya to revert back to doing the things she used to, in the spirit of trying to help. So, she just didn't tell her.

"We had close to a hundred and forty thousand dollars in a black duffle bag, stashed in Marcus's closet. Now, it's not there. So, if you didn't have anyone in the house, what did *you* do with it?

"Me?" Mya looked dejected. Hurt at the implication. "I've never been in Marcus's room. So..." Then it hit her. "Wait! Aunt Meme was here earlier. We were all outside and she asked to use the restroom. But, she didn't have any bag in her hands when she left."

As Ty grilled Mya, Marcus closed his eyes and turned the problem over in his head. Even though he was slow on some things, on others he was almost like a savant. "The back gate!" Both Ty and Meme became quiet. Marcus shook his head as realization hit him. "She threw it out the window. You can't see that part of the house from the driveway. While you were outside with Jeremiah, she came in, opened the window and dropped it into the backyard. Most likely, she doubled back to get it. That's why she didn't have anything in her hands when she left." Once he said it out loud, he knew that was exactly what happened.

"Are you serious?" Mya couldn't believe Meme would do something like that. '*SMACK!*' Ty reached back and slapped fire from Mya. Before she could recover, Ty started beating her like she was just another bitch on the street.

"Bitch. You Let. That. Hoe. Come. Steal. From. Us?" Ty yelled, as she wailed on her daughter. Marcus snatched Ty by her stomach and carried her off while she was kicking and screaming. "Let me go, Marcus. Imma beat that lil hoe's ass. Bitch, you so worried 'bout some dick, you let this grimy ass skeezer steal the money we were saving to get your lil brother back," Ty screamed, just as Marcus dragged her into the master bedroom. He tossed her onto the bed.

"Ty, you need to save some of that for that grimy ass bitch Meme. That was an honest mistake. Mya didn't even know we had that type of money. Maybe if we would've kept her in the loop, she would have known to take better care. We can't take this out on her," Marcus reasoned.

Without no one to punch on, Ty broke down. The tears she was trying to hold back came rushing down like the Niagara Falls. Marcus really didn't know what the next move was. He just knew Ty needed to be held, so that's what he did.

He held on to her until she cried so much, she fell asleep in his arms. After he tucked Ty in, he made his way to go check on Mya. She was back in her room, crying softly. *Knock! Knock! Knock!* Marcus tapped on her bedroom door. "Hey, Mya?" She didn't respond, but he felt she wasn't opposed to him coming in. "I just wanted to tell you, it wasn't your fault."

"What did my momma mean, when she said I let Meme steal the money y'all needed to get CJ back?" Mya asked him without looking back.

Marcus took a couple more tentative steps in, until he was standing next to her bed. After taking a deep breath, he explained. "Well, the people that took your brother had called that same day. They said they wanted two hundred and fifty thousand dollars to give him back. Your mom and I felt we didn't want you worrying about us raising the money. We got it . . . *had* it covered."

That revelation brought a whole new set of tears. "I didn't know. I swear, I didn't know," she cried, as if asking for forgiveness.

"Ssshh . . . It's okay." Marcus took a couple more steps and gave her a great big hug. "We know. Your momma knows. She was just hurt and reacted badly. We know it wasn't your fault."

Even though he was only a couple years older than her, Marcus felt like a full grown man in her arms. His body was hard, but his demeanor was even harder. She held onto him and cried her eyes out. She, too, fell asleep in his arms.

After both ladies of the house were snoring peacefully, Marcus figured he had two days to either try and come up with a quarter million dollars. Or, he could find out where CJ was being held, and try and go get him himself. Marcus grabbed the phone and made a few calls. The streets talked, and it was about time he gave them something to talk about. The Clock was ticking. Sudden death was lurking. He was just hoping for some more overtime.

Chapter 6

"That's a bet, nigga! Matter of fact, I got a hundred say you don't five or nine," Corey challenged Finesse. Both men were on their hands and knees, shooting dice. Every week, a female named Trina and her boyfriend—Coota—held neighborhood dice games. Ten players. Buy in was one thousand dollars apiece.

Both men were sweating. Corey had his shirt off. His wife beater was sticking to his chest. Finesse took his undershirt off and just wore his Houston Rockets jersey. They were the last two gamblers. Corey worked Finesse down to his last couple hundred. If he crapped out here, Corey would be the undisputed winner for the night.

"That's a bet to you, hustler," Finesse responded, before placing his last hundred-dollar chip down. He reared back and let the dice fly. Corey made it seem as if he was going to catch them. Instead, he let them roll. *Four Trey!*

"Don't nobody move but me," Corey shouted, as he raked in the last of the chips.

"Fuck!" Finesse groaned in disappointment. Corey looked at his Cartier. *3:15 a.m.* He hadn't planned on staying that late, but the money was calling. So, he had to answer.

As Finesse left, Trina brought out the money. Ten stacks, to be exact. Corey sat on the couch and counted it. Trina stood with her hands outstretched. By rule, the winner of the dice game had to give the house five hundred dollars.

"Damn, T, you ain't even wait for a nigga to make sure it's all there before you hit my ass up," Corey complained.

"Boy, you know damn well it's all there. That's why you pay us. We make sure everything is on the up and up."

Corey made a show of grudgingly counting out five hundred dollars. He purposely chose to give her all ones, fives and tens. That way, it would take longer.

Trina thought it was to annoy her. Actually, he stalled her out so he could get a longer look at her legendary camel toe. She had her tights jacked up all in her crease. Her sex lips were plump and heavy looking. Trina was slim-thick, with a deep gap between her thighs. Light skin, brown eyes. She was definitely a bad bitch.

"Here you go. Why it always feels like highway robbery when a nigga gotta pay you?" Corey remarked.

"Because it is. Five hundred dollars is nowhere near enough," she spat. Corey smirked, but couldn't take his eyes off her pussy. She knew he was looking. Truth be told, she always made sure she wore something provocative whenever they hosted the dice games.

A lot of dudes came and gambled at their spot. Just to catch a glimpse of the infamous *fat cat*. "Ain't nothing for you down there," she chided him.

Corey couldn't do anything else but lick his lips and shake his head. "That's a damn shame, girl. That motherfucka's like a twenty-dollar hamburger. Let me go before I say or do something that's gonna get us both in trouble."

"Uhh huh," she hurried and showed him to the door.

Stepping outside, Corey felt a light breeze. He didn't bring a jacket or hoodie, because he knew, once he started gambling, things would get hot. He jumped in his Lac, cranked the engine, and made his way out of Riverwood. He turned on Homestead Road and headed back to the East.

Once he got on Tidwell, heading through Verde Forest, he noticed the same pair of headlights had been following him for the last ten minutes. He wasn't sure, but his gut instincts were telling him something wasn't right. He decided to give it a test.

Corey made the right on South Lake Houston Parkway. He traveled all the way down to Highway 90. He turned left, headed to the beltway. Anybody in their right mind would know, taking that route was a waste of time. He could have just rode Tidwell, all the way to the Beltway. That would have saved some time.

So, now that he knew he was being followed, he prepared a trap. *Nigga's trynna jack me? They must have found out I have a lil money,* he figured. Corey made a sharp right into a small neighborhood called Beaumont Place. He knew a few smokers that resided there. Plus, he knew it was a dead end coming up.

He reached under his seat, making sure his Smith and Wesson .357 pistol was cocked and loaded. He turned on the dead end street and before the car could come to a complete stop, he hopped out. *Bocka. Bocka. Bocka. Bocka.*

Corey aimed at the driver side windshield, and let his tool bark. Fire jumped out the barrel of the gun. The front windshield cracked, then shattered. Before the driver of the vehicle could react, the .357 slug penetrated their skull and left them halfway decapitated.

As he approached the car, he could hear a woman's high pitched wail. Then, a familiar name. "Oh my God. Kourtney. Please God, don't let her be dead." *Kourtney?* The only Kourtney Corey knew was his baby momma. But, he knew it couldn't be her. She drove an Altima. This was a Sonata.

Still, he felt a cold dread run through his body. With his pistol at the ready, he approached the driver's side door. His heart dropped. He felt sick. Bile began to rise up through his throat. He was able to choke it back down.

His baby momma, Kourtney, was slumped in the front seat. Half of her head was caved in. Her brains were all over the head rest. One hand still gripped the steering wheel. Her best friend, Liz, couldn't stop screaming. Begging God to perform the greatest miracle man had ever seen.

Corey's knees buckled. He was in a daze as he opened up the driver side door. He noticed Kourtney's other hand held her cell phone. Apparently, she was about to dial his number. "Oh my God! You killed her. You motherfucking murderer. You killed her." Liz began to scream hysterically.

Something about the way she said didn't sit well with Corey. Without too much thought, he upped the pistol and aimed it at her. Liz threw her hands up and screamed like a banshee. *Bocka. Bocka. Bocka.*

Her head snapped, hitting the passenger window with so much force, it left a crack. Blood splattered against it.

Corey ran back to his car, jumped in and reversed. He maneuvered around the parked car with the two bodies in it. His heart leapt out of his chest, his palms clammy as he gripped the steering wheel tightly.

Every time he blinked his eyes, he saw his baby momma's head, blown to bits. He finally began to wonder. *Did anybody see me?* Beaumont Place is a neighborhood filled with smokers. But, that doesn't mean they don't talk to the police. Especially if there's a reward. "Fuck! Fuck! Fuck!" He screamed, banging his head against the steering wheel.

He was trying to figure out, why the hell was she following him around at three o'clock in the morning? Corey didn't even realize it, but tears started to fall, dripping onto his pistol that laid in his lap. He pulled up to his apartment, grabbed some clothes and a few other items, jumped on 59 North, and headed to his kinfolk in Cleveland Texas.

Corey was a city nigga. Born and raised. But, every once in a while, he visited the country. One of his closest relatives was a nigga by the name of Happy. Happy was anything but what his name suggests.

At 5'10, two hundred and forty-five pounds, dark-skinned, with a mean temperament, people usually stayed out of Happy's way. He was mean, but he had an even meaner hustle. When it came to drugs, his motto was, *"If it gets you high, I will supply."*

Corey and Happy's mothers were sisters. Whenever Corey's dad used to get on his drunken raves, him and his mom would shoot up north to Cleveland, Texas. A lot of times, for a week or two. Sometimes, a month or better.

As they got older, Happy and Corey became close. A lot of times, Corey would bring work up to Cleveland. That helped ensure Happy had the town on lock. "What's up, kinfolk?" Happy looked like he was half asleep. Corey showed up at Happy's door in the middle of the night.

"I need a place to crash for a lil bit. I done got into some fluke ass bullshit," Corey tried to explain.

Happy took one look at him, and could tell he needed refuge. "Gone come in." Corey followed him into the house. As he walked in, he noticed Happy's girlfriend, Tee Tee, standing in the kitchen. With a worried look on her face. "It's okay, baby. It's just my cousin Corey," Happy assured her.

Tee Tee wasn't too sure how she felt about that, but she wasn't about to go against Happy's law. Especially not in front of any company. She simply just nodded. "Okay, baby." She excused herself and went back to her room. While Happy was busy looking for the remote, Corey got a glimpse of Tee Tee's backside. She had a serious bump back there.

With skin the color of milk chocolate, big titties, wide hips, she was corn-fed, country-thick. Despite himself, Corey wondered if she had some good pussy. He turned his head back, just in time. "So, what's got you so spooked, my nigga?" Happy wanted to know.

Corey sat down and began to tell Happy everything. He knew Happy was a thorough nigga, so he didn't have to worry 'bout him saying nothing.

"I just need a place to crash for the week. Till all this shit blows over." As he said it, he realized, he really didn't know how long it would take.

"Well, mi casa es tu casa. You'll need to get rid of the Lac in the morning. I got someone that will want to buy it. Also, you'll have to sleep on the couch. You already know, this a one bedroom," Happy laced him up.

"Shit. I ain't tripping, my nigga. I really appreciate it. Matter of fact . . ." Corey pulled out the knot he won at the dice game. "Here go a band." He tried to hand Happy the money.

"I'm good," Happy started to protest.

"Hell naw, my nigga. I know you ain't tripping, but a nigga still gotta pull his weight. You know, I ain't no bum ass nigga." Happy begrudgingly took the money. Then he stood up, ready to head back into the bedroom.

"I gotta finish handling bidness with the misses. I'll catch you in the morning."

"Bet!" With that, Happy left, then returned with a pillow and a blanket. Then, he left again.

Corey laid there, thinking about Kourtney. The boys would be at their grandma's house in Channelview. He didn't know if he could look at them again. Knowing he took their momma away. He fought with himself, trying to get some sleep.

Suddenly, he heard soft moaning coming from the bedroom. Then, the unmistakable sound of skin slapping. "Oh shit, baby. Fuck this pussy. Oh my Gawd! Happy. Just like that. You 'bout to make me cum."

Hearing Happy buss Tee Tee up had Corey's dick on brick. He grabbed at his piece and began to stroke it. He closed his eyes and pictured it was him and not Happy that was knee-deep in Tee Tee's sopping, wet pussy.

He pictured her bent over while he was fucking her. Right in her big, fluffy ass. Minutes later, he came all over his hand. He rushed to the kitchen, grabbed some paper towels, and washed his dick off in the sink. He went and laid back down on the couch. Soon, sleep found him.

Corey thought he heard something. He slowly peeled his eyelids open. He'd almost forgotten where he was at for a second. He checked the clock on the wall. *4:47 a.m.*

Someone was rummaging through the fridge. He peeked his head over the back of the couch, and got a face full of pussy. Tee Tee was bent over, looking for something at the bottom of the fridge. Her baby blue thong was so small, her pussy lips swallowed the crotch area. All you saw was a string between them.

Her pussy hole looked dilated. Corey knew that was courtesy of the beating Happy put on her. His dick was right back rocked up. She stood up and closed the fridge. Corey dropped back down and pretended to be asleep.

Moments later, he felt a presence as she was walking by. Then, she stopped. Corey wanted to open up his eyes, but he knew she was standing over him, watching. He could feel her. He could smell her wet pussy; she was so close. *She must be trynna see if I'm really asleep,* he thought.

Just before Corey worked up enough courage to open his eyes, she continued on into the bedroom. Only then did he peel back his eyelids.

Tee Tee had his mind fucked up and this was only his first night in the house. Now, he was second guessing if it was a good idea for him to be staying there. Shit, but he didn't have anywhere else to go. Hopefully, he won't have to be there long.

Chapter 7

Bo stared at the ceiling, as he laid in his bunk. Thinking. His celly was a 6'3", two hundred and thirty-five pounds Blood, by the name of Time Bomb. Bomb, as they called him, was from a small country town, but moved to Dallas when he was young. Ever since the day Bo moved into the cell, Bomb had been getting *kites* from all his homeboys. Bo could feel the tension.

Being that they were housed on closed custody, they were forced to be in the cell together, twenty-two hours a day. And that's, if they're lucky enough to get rec. Bo was just waiting for something to pop off. He'd left the majority of his property packed up. *Just in case.*

He checked the time on his radio. *6:45 a.m.* The officer on duty was making his initial security check. Time Bomb got out of his bunk and approached the bars. "Say, look out, officer. Y'all running rec today, or what?"

The Nigerian C.O. looked at him with disdain. "No rec . . . Short of staff," he claimed.

"Man, you hoes always talking 'bout *short of staff.* Soon as a nigga go cross one of y'all's shit, it'll be fifty laws down here," Bomb huffed. Being cooped up all day, Rec was the one thing restricted housing inmates had to look forward to. Dudes depended on that rec call, to get off the stress they were dealing with.

Bo could feel Bomb's frustration. "Say, look out celly, you up?"

He leaned over and peered down on Bomb. "Wassup?" Bo asked coldly.

"Can I holla at you, real quick?" Bo jumped off the top bunk and sat on the sink. His back against the wall. He didn't want to strap on his shoes just yet. That would be a declaration that he wanted smoke. Bomb might *just* want to talk. Still, Bo was on point. If Bomb wanted to fuck around, he'd give him what he was looking for. "You drink coffee?"

"Sometimes," Bo answered. "I gotta go to store though. When I got locked up, the bitch ass S.S.I.'s stole a bunch of my shit," Bo told him. It was well-known that if you get locked up and you're not one of the *Guys*, you could be subject to petty theft.

He already knew, since the S.S.I.'s were Bloods, he would get peeled. He was just happy they didn't mess with his hygiene, pictures or legal work. Bomb gave him a knowing look. "Well, I got plenty. If you ever wanna shot, I keep it in the jar, on the floor by the toilet," Bomb offered.

"Bet that." Bo reached into his locker, grabbed his cup, fixed a shot, then sat back down in the same position. Bomb studied him for a few seconds before he spoke.

"What happened with you and the homie up the hallway? They talking 'bout you used a weapon on him." Bo was glad they were finally broaching the subject. He wasn't the type to dance around an issue.

"Naw, fam. I ain't have no weapon. I don't know where they got that shit from. If I used a weapon on dude, I'd be segg'd, not G-5." Bomb nodded to that. Bo continued. "I had this lil bitch on my coat tail. He went back dropping salt on a nigga."

"What the nigga say?" Bomb had already heard the story, but he wanted it from the horse's mouth. Bo figured he already knew, but he welcomed the opportunity to tell his side of the story.

"Dude told her not to fuck with me because I be fucking with punks." Bo tried to read Bomb's reaction. It didn't seem as if he was fazed, so Bo continued. "When I found out, I fell out of place, then stood on my bidness. I don't use weapons, my nigga, I gets mines from the shoulders." Bo threw a light promise out there. He wanted Bomb to know, if *he* ever wanted smoke, Bo would provide the match.

Bomb listened attentively before he spoke. "Yeah, I figured you ain't use no weapon. Like you said, you'd have been in seg, if you did. My only question is . . . Do you fuck around with punks? I mean, that's your dick and that's your bidness, but if we gon' share a cell, I feel like it's a nigga's right to know," Bomb rightfully pointed out.

Bo thought about using an excuse. *I don't have any support out there.* Or, *I got a lot of time, and I was using him for the money.* Instead, he just kept it a *hot dollar.* "Yeah, I fuck around."

Bomb looked at him with new found respect. Even though Bomb didn't promote or participate in homosexuality, he understood that every man has a right to do their time, how they see fit. As long as the respect line isn't crossed, to each his own. "Well, check game, my nigga. I don't fuck around at all. So, I ask that nothing go down in this cell when I'm gone. Other than that, we doing time in this bitch. I got twelve done on a forty, so I ain't going nowhere anytime soon.

Bo nodded. "Yeah, I can dig that, my nigga. I'm all about respect. You ain't gotta worry 'bout none of that. I'm sitting on an L myself."

The two of them began to ride about the world. Where they were from. What they did, or didn't do, to put them in there. After about an hour and a half, the same Nigerian C.O. approached the cell. "Top bunk. Bowman . . . You ready for visit?"

Bo looked at him confused. "Visit? I ain't get no lay-in last night."

"Yeah, sometimes these laws are too lazy to pass them out," Bomb informed him.

"Damn. A'ight then. Give me like five minutes. Let me dress," Bo told the C.O. Once the law left, he took a quick bird bath in the sink, and got himself together.

Since he'd been gone, it's only one person that has come to see him. Even though he felt he already knew who it was, he was still *hoping* it was Ty and the kids.

He walked into visitation, and noticed the stares. He hadn't been on the unit long, and already had three "dubs" under his belt. His name was ringing. Loud and clear. Bo saw his visitor, and couldn't help but smile.

Brown Sugar was rocking a green and white Gucci jumpsuit. Matching high top Gucci sneakers. His wrist glimmered with a simple but elegant, gold Gucci wristwatch. His hands covered in gold and diamond rings. If Bo didn't know any better, Brown Sugar looked like he was pitching big dope. "Heyy, handsome," he cooed.

All of Brown Sugar's thirty-two pearly whites were on display. Snacks covered the counter before him. "Wassup?" Bo asked, as he sat down in the cage. The first time Sugar came to visit him, Bo was a little self-conscious. Always looking around, to see if anyone noticed.

Now, Bo could care less. He was just happy to see his friend. "Wassup, Sug. I see you putting that shit on." Brown Sugar blushed.

"Well, you know me. As sweet as can be . . . What's been up with you? How you holding up?" Brown Sugar asked.

"I'm Gucci, no pun intended." That brought a smile to Sugar's face. "Oh, and thanks for that bread." Brown Sugar made sure Bo's account stayed fat. Every month, two hundred and fifty to three hundred dollars got deposited to his trust fund. It would have been more, but they would have frozen his account. Brown Sugar wanted to make sure Bo had everything he wanted and needed.

Bo had just been fucking with Rose, so he wouldn't have to spend his own money. Or at least, that's what he told himself. "Boy, you know I got you. I told you, as long as I'm out here, you're good."

Ever since they were neighbors in the county, Brown Sugar made sure Bo was well taken care of. "I got some good news. I found a lawyer that's interested in your case." Bo's ears perked up. He sat up straight, eager to hear more.

"Oh yeah, what they talkin' 'bout?"

"He went ahead and looked into it. He said he checked out the offense report. Supposedly, the store clerk had said something different the night off. But, your trial lawyer didn't impeach him. He also told me about three or four more different errors. Long story short, he's talking like he's going to bring you home."

Bo bubbled with excitement. This was the best news he'd had since he'd been locked up. Then, it dawned on him. He was broke. How was he going to pay for the services? He doubted Brown Sugar was *really* going to pay all that money.

"What? Is he *pro bono*?" Bo asked.

Brown Sugar looked at him as if he just said he'd been born a woman. "Boy, stop playing. You know damn well these big lawyers ain't doing shit for free. Unless it benefits them. He's charging forty thousand dollars."

Bo's face fell. That might as well be a million dollars right now. He didn't have shit, but what was on his account. Even though that was enough to make sure he was kept fed, paying for a lawyer was a whole other ball game.

Brown Sugar noticed his look of disappointment. "Why you looking all sad and shit? I already dropped off 10k to him yesterday." Bo's face lit up. He couldn't believe it. Brown Sugar was a blessing from God. Never in a million years would he have thought he'd have genuine love for a gay man.

Bo was speechless. He wanted to give him a hug and kiss him on the cheek. "Imma make some moves next month, then I'll drop the other thirty on him," Sugar explained.

"Sugar. I don't know what to say. I mean—" Brown Sugar cut him off.

"Look, Bo. I know when we first met, you didn't know what to expect from me. The truth is, I love you. I've been *in* love with you for some time now. I want you to come home to me. You don't have to make a decision right now. Regardless, your lawyer will be paid for. I want to spend the rest of my life taking care of you."

Bo didn't know how to respond. He honestly had strong feelings for Sugar. Feelings he didn't know he could possess for another man. *Could he actually go home to him? What would his kids say?* Then again, didn't he owe Brown Sugar at least that? A shot at seeing what could be?

To say he was confused was an understatement. The rest of the visit was spent with them laughing and talking shit. When the time was up, Brown Sugar stood up, then blew Bo a kiss. "I love you."

Bo couldn't help himself. "I love you too, Sugar." And, he meant it. Bo was led back to his block in handcuffs. His mind was on Brown Sugar, and how he was almost free. Because of him, and him alone.

Chapter 8

After months of being locked in a cage like an animal, Calvin "Chief" Sage was finally released from the county jail. Marcus kept his word. The rat nigga—Keon—was no longer a problem.

At two hundred pounds. Solid muscle. He was twenty pounds heavier than when he went in. Waves on three hundred and sixty degrees, Tsunami status. Chief went from a boy to a man. In a matter of months.

He couldn't wait to blow a blunt and fall into some tight, wet pussy. As he walked up out of the county, his mom was there to pick him up. Like he knew she would be. Chief was definitely a momma's boy. Laura was his world, and he would kill behind her and Cindy.

As soon as she laid eyes on him, she hopped out to give him a great, big 'welcome home' hug. Chief stopped her dead in her tracks and frowned. "Momma. What the hell you got going on?" Laura had on a pair of cotton shorts so small, her pussy lips could clearly be seen. The crack of her ass was chewing on the material. It looked as if the shorts were painted on.

Her lavender top was just as small. With no bra, her genetically enhanced breasts stood up. Perky. Nipples, hard as granite. She looked down at herself. "What you mean, what I got going on?"

Chief pointed to her outfit. "*All this*. Momma, why you come out the house looking like that? You gone make me have to kill one of these perv ass niggas out here."

"Boy, hush. Your momma grown. I look good and I'm proud of it. Now, give me a hug." She reached out and grabbed a hold of him. Chief caught a whiff of her fragrance. She smelled like cinnamon and roses. He missed her scent. His mom always smelt the way a woman should.

They were on I-10, headed East. Chief saw Frenchy's. His stomach instantly began to growl. "Momma. Stop at Frenchy's real quick."

"Boy, you know I cooked something for you. I'm not about to have you eating fast food on your first day out of jail."

Chief wanted to protest. It was no use. Plus, he knew his mom could throw down in the kitchen. So, whatever she had on the stove would hit the spot.

When they pulled up to the house, Chief noticed a black Toyota sitting in the driveway. "Whose car is that?"

"Oh. That's your sister's friend, Taylor."

"Taylor? Who's that? I don't know no Taylor," Chief asked, interested.

"That's because your sister just started hanging with her. Two months ago." Soon as they walked into the house, Cindy jumped up, ran and crashed into him for a hug.

She leaned back, appraising him. "Damn, boy. Your ass got big ass hell," she said, while holding him at arm's length. She looked him up and down, admiring his physique. Chief caught Taylor admiring him from the corner of her eye.

Taylor looked to be about 5'4", one hundred and thirty pounds. Banana red complexion. Nice bubble butt, with some wide hips. Even though she had some small B cup titties, she could definitely get it.

Once him and Cindy were done getting reacquainted, he gave Taylor his full attention. "And... *Who* is this?" Taylor was twenty years old, but around the younger Chief, she seemed shy as hell.

Cindy took charge of the greeting. "Boy. This my girl, Taylor. Taylor, this my brother Calvin."

"Nice to meet you, Calvin." Chief looked at his sister, annoyed, before turning back towards Taylor.

"Don't nobody call me Calvin, but these two." He motioned to his mom and his sister. "All my friends call me Chief. You wanna be my *friend*?"

Before she could answer, Cindy grabbed ahold of her hand. "No. She doesn't want to be your friend. She's already *my* friend. Find your own friends," Cindy curtly said.

Chief threw up his hands in mock surrender, as Cindy pulled Taylor away and into her bedroom. He got a good look at Taylor from the back. Her booty cheeks jiggled, with each step she took. He felt his dick twitch, as he tried to guess how good her pussy must feel.

Later that evening, he ate dinner with his mom and sister. Due to Cindy's orders, Taylor ate her plate in her room. Chief was trying to figure out why his sister was so D'd up when it came to Taylor. It wasn't like he wanted to be her friend for real. He just wanted to dig up in her guts a couple times, then send her on her way.

After dinner, he called Marcus up. Of course, Marcus was excited to hear his best friend was finally free. He filled him up on what had been going on since he'd left. How he had gone in and bought a house with his *old school*. Chief couldn't wait to see it.

They made plans for the following day. Marcus would come scoop him up, so they could kick it. Once they hung up the phone, Chief grabbed some weed he'd stolen out of his mom's stash earlier, a cigar, and twisted one up. *Knock. Knock. Knock.* "Come in."

Laura poked her head into his room. "I'm 'bout to go out tonight. I won't be back until morning. I left a hundred dollars on the kitchen counter. If you need me to pick up anything while I'm gone, just text me, and I'll get it on the way home. A'ight? And don't smoke up all my shit either."

"A'ight, momma. I got you," Chief said exasperatedly.

"Yeah, you got me alright. You got me messed up." Chief shook his head as his momma closed his bedroom door. It had been months since he smoked some good weed. In the County, dudes were smoking K-2. He wasn't about to mess with that. He'd heard dudes were spraying roach spray and rat poison on it. Chief wasn't about to go out like that.

The first blunt to the head put him on his ass. The last thing he remembered was: putting on the movie *Friday*. Before it got to the part where Craig got fired on his day off, Chief was out like a light.

A couple of hours later, he awoke. He felt like he could eat a horse. In nothing but a pair of basketball shorts, he ventured off into the kitchen. He passed up his sister's bedroom, and felt he must've still been high. It sounded like someone was moaning.

He leaned in. Put his ear to the door. "Ooh, ssshit! You finna make me cum, baby," Cindy moaned. *That's why she was so D'd up. They're fucking.*

Chief didn't even know his sister messed around with girls. Even though it was his sister in there, he wanted to see Taylor in action. He pictured her on her hands and knees. Ass tooted in the air. Her pussy slick and splayed open as she feasted on Cindy's box. His dick became rocked up.

He reached into his shorts, pulled out his piece, and began stroking until he was at his full potential. He closed his eyes and pictured Taylor with her tongue deep in Cindy's ass crack. He imagined hitting Taylor from the back, while his sister rode her face. If two brothers could flip a chick, why not a brother and a sister?

Chief reached for the door handle. *Locked.* Forced to stand outside the door. Dick in hand. Listening to his sister cum all over Taylor's face.

His balls popped. Cum shot all over the bedroom door, months of built up frustration dripping down onto the carpet. The nut was so intense, he began to get light-headed. Woozy. He staggered to the kitchen, washed his hands, then fixed himself something to eat.

After devouring a sandwich, he decided to smoke one in the backyard. He grabbed some weed out of his room and on his way back out, he bumped into Taylor. Coming out of Cindy's bedroom. '*Ooff!*' "My bad," he apologized.

Chief took one look at her. His jaw dropped. Taylor was in nothing but a yellow, bumble bee thong. A small, yellow and white tee, with a picture of a unicorn on it. He was so close, he could smell his sister's pussy on her face. "Naw. That's my bad," she corrected. "I should have watched where I was going."

She glanced down at his print. Chief's dick began to rise. Now that he was face to face with her, he was stuck. Speechless. "Uh. Uhm . . . I was heading to the restroom," she pointed out. Chief hadn't realized he was blocking her path.

"Oh. My bad. Excuse me." Chief stepped out of the way and watched Taylor's ass bounce and jiggle the whole way to the bathroom. He walked towards the door, placing his ear against it. He could hear her pee tinkling, as she relieved her bladder.

He hurried back to his sister's bedroom. He wanted to see what Taylor was on, but he didn't need Cindy causing a scene. He twisted her door knob slowly. The door creaked open, slightly.

Laying on the bed face down, passed out, with nothing but a sheet covering her lower half, was Cindy. Chief listened to her snore lightly. He hurriedly but quietly closed the door and made his way back to the bathroom.

Chief twisted the door knob. Taylor was still seated on the toilet. Her panties were down to her shins. Her elbows were resting on her knees. She saw him, and quickly sat up. "Uh-Uh. Boy, what you doing?" she asked him, perturbed.

He threw his hands up. "It ain't nothing like that. I just wanted a chance to get at you, without my sister being around. I know y'all got y'all own thing going." She looked abashed. "I overheard y'all," he clarified for her. "But look. I'm fresh out. I ain't had no pussy in months. I'm digging your lil vibe. I'm trynna see if you could bless a nigga with some of that. You got my word, my sister will never know."

As he was making his pitch, he was inching closer and closer until he was only a mere few feet away. Taylor looked up at him, her eyes cutting towards the door.

Chief sensed her trepidation. He reached back and locked it. She bit her bottom lip as he took two more steps toward her. With trembling hands, she reached up, grabbed his waistband and pulled down. His hefty sized cock flopped out, hanging inches away from her face.

Taylor grabbed ahold of him, her small hands warm and clammy to the touch. She tilted her head back, opened wide, and dropped the tip of his dick into her mouth.

Chief moaned, grabbing the back of her skull, easing himself deeper down her throat. Taylor grabbed the sides of his hips and steadied herself. *Ghlup. Ghlup. Ghlup.* His dick head was scraping the back of her throat. Chief pushed through, while he pulled her back, forcing her to deep-throat most of his cock.

She began to tap on his thighs. He pulled back. "Aaahhh-huuuh." She took in a great, huge breath, ropes of saliva hanging from her lip, to the tip of his dick.

"Stand up," he ordered. With her panties still wrapped around her shins, she stood up and turned around. Taylor gripped the toilet tank, her banana red pussy lips wet and meaty. Chief dropped down and stuck his tongue in her pussy hole. Her booty smelled fresh. He couldn't resist. His tongue slid up and down her ass crack.

Taylor shivered, bit her lip, while he bottom-fed. Once he felt she was good and ready, Chief stood tall, lined himself up, and plunged deep into her womb.

She jerked forward. One hand against the wall. The other, gripping the toilet tank. He held her hips tightly. Gave it to her hard. Her coochie began to talk to him, squelching, as Chief continued to beat her walls loose. He delivered the type of force and pressure she'd never experienced.

He slammed the lid down on the seat, and pushed her forward, allowing her to sit her knees on the toilet lid. "Ooh shit. Ooh shit. This too much dick. I can't take it. I can't take it. It's too much," Taylor panted and protested. Chief slapped her on the ass, then pulled back.

His dick slid and flopped out. "Get on the sink." Taylor climbed aboard, her legs wide, her back against the mirror, panties hanging off one ankle. She gripped the back of her thighs and prepared for impalement.

She looked down at Chief's salami sized cock, as it spread her sex lips apart. "Aggh, fuuckk. Sssht!" She moaned as he buried himself to the hilt.

For the next twenty minutes, he fucked her like she stole from him. When it was time for him to cum, he backed up. Taylor hopped off the counter, dropped to her knees, just as the first spurt shot from his dick head. She drank him up greedily, each spurt met with a huge gulp. "Dammmnn. Fuuucckk. Shit, girl," Chief groaned, as Taylor continued to suck him dry. Smacking her lips afterwards.

She lifted his shaft, and licked under his ball sack. Chief looked down at her in amazement. She was definitely worth the risk. He palmed her forehead with his left hand, and pried her away from his dick.

He grabbed himself and squeezed until the last few drops peeked out of his piss hole. Chief dabbed it off on her tongue and then watched as she rubbed her tongue all over her cum-stained teeth. "Shit, girl, that pussy and head too good for you to be *just* fucking with bitches," Chief told her exhaustedly.

Taylor slipped her panties back on, fixed herself and said, "I'm Bi. I could never give up dick completely. I'm your sister's first. I guess you can say, *I* turned her out."

"Okay, well, check it. Is you gon' let a nigga get some of that from time to time? I'm not trynna fuck up what you and my sister got going. But, if you gon' be around, we might as well sneaky link from time to time."

Taylor looked unsure. "I don't know, man. I don't want to hurt your sister. Look, let's just see what it do. I'm not gonna promise anything. But, if we bump into each other, and it's the right place and the right time. Then, we can get active. Till then, *this* never happened."

"For shit sho," Chief agreed before walking out of the bathroom. As he walked by her door, Cindy emerged out of her bedroom, dressed in a purple robe that was tied at the waist. Instead of keeping on to his room, he made a turn and headed to the kitchen. He grabbed a soda, some chips, and the hundred his mom left on the counter. Then, he headed back to his bedroom.

Right as he got to his door, he witnessed his sister and Taylor locked in a passionate kiss. *I hope she brushed her teeth,* he thought, as he shut the door behind him.

Chapter 9

J Wright was getting tired of babysitting duty. Yesterday, he made a week flat. CJ was still in his custody. Carleen seemed as if she was starting to get attached. J Wright definitely wasn't feeling that. If it was up to him, he would've just stuffed the little brat into the closet until it was time to get paid.

Speaking of getting paid, Pat *still* hadn't dropped off the bag yet. He picked up the phone and dialed Pat's number again. Still, no answer. *He better not try and jack me. Big homie or not, Imma spank his ass,* J Wright thought to himself, as he toyed with his Glock 18.

CJ walked into the living room, timidly. He was frightened of the man with the gun. Each day, he would say his prayers, asking God to make Aunt Meme come get him. She said she would, and she had always told him the truth. He was hungry—so, so hungry.

It had been two days since he'd eaten. Carleen is the only one that feeds him. But, she was rarely home. Even though neither her or J Wright were allowed to leave, that was a rule she broke often. So, CJ was alone in the house with J Wright.

He stood there trembling, afraid to speak, but needing to eat something. "Excuse . . . Excuse me sir," He said, his tiny voice struggling to be heard. "Can. Can I please have something to eat. I'm hungry," CJ pleaded.

He'd lost ten pounds since he'd been there. For a little boy his age, that's quite a drastic change. J Wright looked at him with a sneer. "If you don't sit your lil punk ass down somewhere, you'll never see your mommy again."

That was the threat that always drove little CJ back to his hiding place in the closet. The only place in the whole house where he felt safe. When he was in there, they never messed with him. Sometimes, he even thought that they'd forgotten about him. He only came out when he needed to eat. Or, when he needed to use the restroom.

Carleen gave him a bath once, but he didn't like it. He didn't know her. It felt strange, since it wasn't his momma or Meme. His stomach began to tie in knots. The pain was beginning to be too much. He cried as he clutched his tummy.

He was so hungry. So scared. With tears in his eyes, he begged. "Momma, please come get me. Please. I'll be a good boy. I promise, I won't be bad anymore."

J Wright sat at the table pissed. He told himself, if Pat didn't call him by the end of the day, he was going to get rid of the kid. One way or another. Suddenly, his phone lit up. He looked at the screen. The number was blocked. He almost didn't answer. *Fuck it!*

"Hello? Yeah. Why you called me blocked? A'ight. So wait, I'm still getting my bread. Right? A'ight. Well, let me take care of that, and I'll meet you at the spot. A'ight, Yeah." J Wright hung up the phone. Relieved, but at the same time anxious. *Finally, it's time to get rid of the lil brat,* he thought.

He grabbed his car keys and walked in the room where they kept CJ hidden. At first, he thought maybe he'd escaped. There was no sign of him. He checked under the bed. *Nothing.* When he found him laying curled up in the closet, he breathed a sigh of relief. "Get up," he nudged CJ with the toe of his sneaker.

CJ woke up frightened. He scrambled backwards, slinking away, thinking the man with the gun was going to hit him. "Let's go. Imma take you to go see your momma." CJ's eyes lit up. His little heart couldn't beat any faster.

Relief and joy flooded his little body. He shook and trembled with excitement. CJ ran out the room, and waited at the front door. There was no way he was going to miss this ride. "Here. Put this on," J Wright told him, as he threw him an oversized Starter Jacket. After CJ slipped on the jacket, they made their way to the car.

He was so weak he couldn't even open the car door. J Wright had to come around and open it for him. He watched as CJ climbed in. As they drove, CJ stared at the stores and the lights passing by. It was dark out. It didn't matter. CJ wasn't scared anymore. He was going home. Then, he noticed the buildings started to disappear. There were less and less lights. It looked the same, as when he used to go visit his "Paw Paw" in the country. A lot of grass, and almost no lights.

He felt something terrible pass through his body. His heart galloped in his chest. *The man said he was taking me to go see momma. Would he lie for no reason?*

CJ's leg began to bounce. His teeth began to chatter. He felt he needed to pee. He didn't know what to do. Something in his head kept screaming for him to just open up the door and jump out. But the car was going too fast. He checked his sweaty hands.

Finally, they pulled over and stopped. J Wright told him to "get out".

"But. But, I don't see my momma," CJ stuttered. His hands trembled, as he reached for the door handle. "Please sir. I just wanna go home. I didn't do anything bad. Please," he begged.

"Boy. Get out the car. Your momma's just over there." CJ looked towards where he pointed. He knew the man was lying. He was scared to get out of the car, but he knew if he didn't, the man would hurt him.

CJ reluctantly pulled the door handle with all his little strength. The door popped open. He damn near fell out. As he stepped out, J Wright was right behind him. CJ noticed the gun in his hand. This time, he was holding it differently.

He wanted to be brave like his daddy, but he was so scared. He took a couple steps into the dark field. He looked back at J Wright. Tears began to pour from his eyes. He knew he would never see his momma again. Never will he get to watch movies and eat snacks with Mya while momma was gone. "Please. I'm sorry. Whatever I did, I'm sorry."

J Wright was stone-faced. "Keep walking. You'll be home soon," he told him as he pointed the gun towards little CJ, urging him along.

"Momma. Where are you? Please come get me, momma. I'm sorry. Do you love me, momma? Please come." CJ cried, as he begged the heavens for his momma.

J Wright leveled the Glock at the back of CJ's head. *Bocka!* All it took was one shot, for such a small body. The back of his head caved in. The hollow point exited through his forehead. Leaving everything, from his jawline to the top of his crown, detached.

His small body dropped like a sack of potatoes. J Wright went back to the car and grabbed three, heavy-duty Hefty trash bags. Per request, he stuffed the frail, lifeless corpse into the bags, tied them up, then headed back into town. Pat wanted to send a message.

He had J Wright dump the body in a dumpster behind the restaurant he took Ty to when they first went out. *Her favorite one.*

Afterwards, J Wright drove to a disclosed location. To collect his money. Ten bands for watching and ten bands for disposing.

He pulled up to the address. The street was pitch-black. It seemed some of the kids in the hood busted out the street lights. J Wright sat idly in the car. Even though he shouldn't have had anything to worry about, he kept his Glock sitting on his lap. Right next to the phone.

He checked the time. Pat was ten minutes late, *as usual.* He told himself this would be the last time he put in work for Pat. *The nigga doesn't even do shit when he's supposed to.* J Wright was extremely disgruntled.

Just then, his phone rang. Once again, it was from a blocked call. Figuring it must be Pat, he answered. "Hello? Yeah, I'm at the spot. Right here on . . ." *Pfft. Pfft. Pfft.*

Silenced shots chewed through the driver side window. Lead connected with J Wright's left temple and traveled through his right, leaving his phone with a hole and a cup of blood on it.

There was no way Pat was going to allow J Wright to live. Not after he ordered him to kill a little boy. He really expected Ty to pay the ransom. When she didn't, his hand was forced. He couldn't damn well just give the boy back for free. *Ain't no stupid shit!*

So now, Pat had to tie up *all* loose ends. That's why he had them snatch up the smoker Carleen earlier that day. As J Wright lay dead in the front seat, his henchmen stuffed the body of the dead dope fiend in the trunk of his car. They dropped one of little CJ's belongings, the nerf football Meme had brought him, in the car with them. When the cops discover it, they'll head back to the house and find all types of DNA evidence. Now, Pat just had to figure out what to do with Meme.

Ty was pacing back and forth in her room, staring nervously at her phone. The deadline was two days ago. She wasn't able to pay the ransom. The calls had suddenly stopped. Ty wished desperately that she could call them and beg them for more time. She had no idea who she should call.

Marcus had been going hard. Coming and going, all throughout the night. Each time, bringing home money, then heading right back out. Ty would often see blood splatters on his clothes. He would take a second to change into something else before he headed back out the door. Without being told to, Ty would bleach, then destroy the evidence.

He barely said a word. Ty sensed he was too scared to stop. Holding on to hope—that if he kept hitting, eventually he would have enough and the kidnappers would call and give them one more chance to pay.

She'd never been a praying woman. But, these last few days, Ty'd been on her knees, asking the good Lord to save her only son. *Her baby boy.* She couldn't understand who would do this to him. A child. One that wouldn't hurt a mouse. One that would rather shoo a roach away instead of stomping it with a shoe.

Mya had been in her room, refusing to come out. Ty would often overhear her crying on the phone. No doubt, to her boyfriend. Constantly asking him, why? The same question Ty had been asking herself all week.

All she could do now was stare at her phone as it sat on the dining room table. Suddenly, it began to ring. The tone was Marcus's. She quickly answered it. "Hello?"

"Hey. I'm 'bout to swing through. I got my homie Chief with me. He agreed to help us look for CJ," Marcus informed her.

"Okay. I'll be home."

"You need something, baby?" he asked her.

"My son, Marcus. I need my baby boy." Ty fought back tears. She needed to be strong. To cry would be to admit all was lost.

"We'll get him back, babe. We'll find him," Marcus tried to reassure her. They talked for a few more minutes, then disconnected the call.

Half an hour later, Chief and Marcus walked through the front door. Ty took notice of the young man. If it was another time and place, she might have taken pause at how attractive he was.

It was hard to believe, the two of them were so young. Both eighteen, but built like men ten to fifteen years their senior. Marcus made the introductions before dropping the money off in the safe in his room. Ever since Meme, he'd made sure everything was locked and secured.

Marcus went back downstairs, fixed himself a drink as Ty stood motionless, staring at her phone. "I assume, still nothing," he said. She shook her head by way of saying *no*. Not once taking her eyes off the phone. "Look, Ty, Chief and I are about to comb the streets. Is there anything you could think of that could help?"

Ty'd been racking her brain, trying to think of something. No matter how hard she tried, her mind always came up blank. She thought maybe it was one of the past licks Marcus and her had hit. But, none of them knew where she lived. Plus, most of them were dead and gone.

Her, Marcus and Chief, stood around the kitchen table, tossing ideas around. "Momma. Momma. Turn on the news!" Mya yelled frantically. Ty's body froze over. Her heart seemed to have paused, neglecting to beat for more than a few seconds, her lungs refusing to pull in oxygen. She couldn't breathe. She grabbed the remote. Her hands shook as she turned on the news.

A middle-aged black female reporter stood in front of Ty's favorite Mexican restaurant. Ty turned the volume all the way up.

"Today is truly a sad day for humanity. Earlier this morning, workers at this Mexican restaurant were emptying out the trash and came across a strange garbage bag. According to the workers, the restaurant uses white bags, and the trash bag that was discovered was a black one. Upon further inspection, they discovered the trash bag had a small, unidentified boy's body in it. Police are asking for your help in identifying the victim. If you have any questions, please call 713..."

Ty sat there, shaking her head. She didn't believe it. *Couldn't believe it.* It had to be someone else's baby boy. But somehow, she knew it was her CJ. "Do you want me to call?" Somehow, Marcus's words broke through her thoughts.

She snapped out of her daze. She looked aimlessly around. Mya sat on the bottom of the stairs, crying. Marcus didn't know what to do or say to console either one of them. Ty just nodded.

Marcus dialed the number. Forty-five minutes later, they were pulling up to the city morgue to identify the body. Before they walked in, Ty said a quick prayer. The lead investigator on the case, as well as the Chief Coroner, met them at the front desk. "Follow this way," the coroner said, as he walked towards the back of the building.

He was a white-haired, middle-aged white man. He wore a pair of thick-rimmed glasses and had a pot belly that hung below his waist line. The detective, a thirty-something-year-old black male, had a bald head and a goatee, with smooth, milk chocolate skin. He approached and asked for their identification. After jotting down their info, he escorted them to the back.

As they approached the table, the white sheet laid heavily on the small lifeless body. Ty's knees buckled. Her teeth chattered. Her rib cage ached from her rapidly beating heart.

The detective, who they later learned was named Alfred, pulled the sheet back. Mya screamed. Ty fainted into Marcus's arms. *There it was.* Her innocent baby boy, with half his head blown off. Marcus nodded to the detective. Confirmation.

He covered the body back up and gave the family time to gather themselves. Eventually, they were able to face reality. After a long talk with detectives, Ty went ahead and confessed. She told them she knew her son had gotten kidnapped. Right in front of their house, but she was attempting to pay the ransom. They asked her if she thought she knew who the kidnappers were. *If I did, I wouldn't be standing here talking to you. It would have been one of their family members coming to identify them,* she thought to herself.

Detectives chastised her for not coming forth sooner. They explained that they might have been able to save him if they had the time, information and resources. Ty and her family made the long and dreadful ride home.

When they pulled up, Chief was outside, smoking a blunt. He had suggested staying back. He felt like the viewing was a family matter. Even though he and Marcus were like brothers, he didn't feel like it would have been appropriate.

Ty was the first to step out, with her head down, feet dragging as she made her way to the front door. Mya appeared next. After her initial outburst, she found her strength and composed herself. She even helped Marcus subdue and comfort Ty. As Mya passed Chief up, they locked eyes. He gave her a reassuring smile. She returned the gesture.

As Marcus approached, Chief reached in his pocket and pulled out a pre-rolled cigarillo. "Here. I figured you might need this," he said as he passed it to Marcus. He accepted it, put a flame to the tip and pulled. After four good hits, he felt his stress melt away. "Damn, nigga," Chief began. "I guess sometimes it's better to be in jail than to be out here. Dealing with this type of shit."

Marcus handed him the blunt back. "Dawg. Lil man ain't never hurt nobody. Crazy thing is, he was probably going to be the only one to grow up and really do something." His eyes began to mist. He took a deep breath, then shook his head. "On me. Whoever did this . . . is gonna pay. I don't give a fuck," Marcus growled.

"We gon' make them pay, together." Chief concurred. The two friends continued to smoke and drink until the wee hours of the morning, eyelids heavy, barely able to speak.

"Damn. What time is it?" Marcus asked. They were so caught up, time passed them by. It was after 1:00 a.m.

Marcus was in no position to drive. "Say, bro, you ain't trippin 'bout spending the night, is you? I'll take you home in the morning," he slurred.

Chief didn't mind at all. The two went inside. Marcus retired to Ty's bedroom. "If you want, you can take the couch. Or, you can sleep in my bed," he told Chief, before closing the door behind him.

Marcus needed to make sure Ty would be alright for the night. Ever since they left the morgue, Ty barely spoke. When she did, it was monotone.

He walked in and noticed her curled up under the covers. With the steady rhythm of her breath, only the blanket moved. Marcus stripped down to his boxers, crawled into bed and held her. She fell asleep in his arms.

Chief stretched out on the couch, flipping through the channels. He stripped off his True Religion shirt and jeans. He laid there in nothing but a pair of basketball shorts and a crispy white, wife beater.

As he was preparing to doze off, he thought he heard footsteps coming down the stairs. He resisted the urge to open up his eyes. He knew it was Mya. Ty and Marcus were laid up in the master bedroom, downstairs.

He listened as she disabled the alarm and tiptoed on the tile, in the foyer. The door creaked open. After some hushed whispers, the door closed. Chief could hear two sets of footsteps. Shuffling, quickly by. *Damn, she a freak. She done snuck someone over*, he thought, as he laid there, pretending to be asleep.

Once he heard them ascend up the stairs, he peeked over the back of the couch. Chief caught the backs of Mya and some nigga. Mya's ass was sitting fat in a pair of mesh boy shorts. His dick began to rock up. He wondered if Marcus had sampled the momma *and* the daughter.

He got up and crept over to Ty's door. He put his ear up to it, and listened. He heard the soft snores. *Good. They're sleep.*

Chief crept up the stairs. He got to the room he figured was Mya's. He leaned in, but couldn't hear much. He slowly twisted the knob and nudged it open. With only a slither of space, he got quite a sight. Mya was already naked, on her hands and knees, hovering over dude's dick.

Her pussy was fat as hell. From his vantage point he could tell her coochie had a couple miles on it. Her hole was slightly dilated. Her sex lips were sort of haggard. Her titties shook, as she bobbed up and down on dude's cock.

Chief caught a glimpse of the dude's face. Recognition hit him. *Jeremiah?* He knew him from school.

Jeremiah was a football standout, who thought he was big shit because his uncle pushed big dope. Chief was messing with a girl named Roxanne. One day, he overheard Roxanne telling one of her friends how she was planning on giving Jeremiah some pussy.

Of course, the Chief dumped her on the spot. Now, he could get his lick back. He was already eyeing Mya. This was just a bigger reason for him to buss her ass up,

Chief watched her work that dick for another ten minutes, then crept back downstairs. *Imma get my chance,* he told himself. *Let the nigga think he's doing something.* By the time Chief would be done with Mya, she wouldn't even remember Jeremiah's name.

Chapter 10

"Say, kinfolk, look in the glovebox. See if you see some blunt wraps in there," Happy told Corey, as they traveled down a dark, country road. Corey popped the glove box open. Sure enough, two blunt wraps almost fell out. "Here. Twist one up." Happy tossed him a sack of Loud. Corey wasted no time rolling it.

They pulled up to a yellow, wooden house in the middle of nowhere. It was jam-packed. People were everywhere, drinking, smoking, having a good ole country time.

Earlier that day, Happy asked Corey if he wanted to hit up a house/field party. Corey was hesitant at first. The last thing he needed was to be out and about, especially when the laws were out looking for him back in the city.

Reluctantly, he agreed. After Happy told him he was guaranteed to fall in some pussy, of course. "Kinfolk. You from Houston. Soon as these bitches hear that, they gon' be all over ya ass," he claimed.

Corey wanted to jump fly and put that shit on, but Happy told him that was a bad idea. "Bruh. This a house party in the country. So that means, lots of grass, lots of dirt and lots of bugs. Keep that shit simple. I'm going white tee, shorts, with some Cool Gray J's. Make no mistake, though, my neck and wrist gon' glitter," he boasted.

Happy rocked a charm, and encrusted Jesus piece, with a yellow gold, buss down Rolex. Since it was dark out, any light that hit his jewels seemed to make them dance even brighter.

Corey followed suit, rocking a pair of Levi shorts, with a black wife beater. Some black and gold, Lebron 6's. He threw on the only jewelry he was able to grab, when he went to the house. A Cuban link, with the matching bracelet and a customized TV Johnny watch.

They parked in a field on the side of the house. Happy's rims would surely be dusty when morning came. As they were walking up the driveway, a short, thick, chocolate female with big titties, but a flat booty, approached. She was happy and obviously drunk. "Heyy, Happy. I'm surprised your ass showed up. You know, Tee Tee don't ever let you out her sight."

"There you go, Deedra. Every time I see you, you got Tee Tee in your mouth."

"Well. Maybe that's because you always got a bitch's mouth empty," she boldly stated. Happy looked at her, then looked at the house. It seemed as if he was weighing his options.

Deedra must have won the coin toss, because Happy grabbed her hand and led her off somewhere. Corey looked at Happy leaving, with annoyance. He couldn't believe it. They hadn't even set foot in the party, and he was already being abandoned. He looked around. He wasn't about to be left standing out there looking like a fool.

He decided to push on, and made his way into the party. The inside of the house felt like it was ten degrees hotter than the outside. Liquor flowed freely. The stereo system was bumping Moneybagg Yo. Females were twerking, while dudes were trying to stick their hands up their coochies.

Corey felt out of place. He literally didn't know anyone there. He edged his way into the kitchen. A big burly black dude with a nappy fro and pugged nose was pouring people drinks out of an ice cooler filled with liquor and fruit juice.

He grabbed a cup and ventured into the backyard. Which happened to be an acre of land that was fenced in. Horses and cows could be seen a hundred yards in the distance. Corey smelled the sweet scent of weed in the air. He snapped and realized he still had the sack of weed Happy threw at him. Plus, the last blunt wrap. *Fuck it! Happy just gon' have to be mad,* he thought, as he twisted up.

After hitting it a couple times, a redbone, slim chick with short hair and light brown eyes approached. Corey licked his lips, eyeing her up and down. Her white shorts were creeping up her crevices, her camel toe on full display. Her blue and white tee was a size too small. She also had that gap all slim chicks have.

She just stood there. Corey knew she was waiting on him to say something. He took the bait. "Excuse me. Excuse me." He had to speak loud enough for her to hear over the music. She turned, a half smile plastered on her face.

The female looked at the blunt. "What you smoking? I don't do reggie."

Corey looked at her with amusement. "Reggie? I don't smoke shit, if it isn't the Za . . . Here." He handed her the blunt.

She took a deep pull. After coughing up a lung, she nodded her approval, then passed it back to him. "Whoooh. That's some gas right there," she exclaimed. Still trying to catch her breath. "Damn!"

Corey smirked. "Let me find out. You talk that big girl shit, but you need a car seat."

"Oh, trust, baby boy. I can hang. The question is, do *you* hang?" She glanced at his crotch suggestively. *Damn. These country girls are freaked the fuck out,* Corey thought. His piece began to respond to her advances. He could definitely get used to the country life.

"Oh, trust and believe. A nigga can *hang* out all night. Matter of fact, where can we go to talk in private? I ain't with all this." He gestured towards the crowded party atmosphere.

She bit her lip and said, "Follow me". The female led him through the party and out a side door. The whole time, Corey had his eyes glued to her nice, little bubble butt. He estimated, she probably weighed about 120 lbs. Tops. He would definitely have fun tossing her around.

They walked out the side door, and ventured down the street. After three minutes of walking, Corey had to ask. "Say, lil momma. Where we going?"

"It's a middle school up ahead. We gon' kick it over there," she told him over her shoulder.

Something wasn't sitting right with Corey. Now, he regretted the fact that he didn't have his strap with him. He'd figured that since he was with his cousin, he didn't need it. But now, he wasn't so sure.

Corey contemplated turning around and going back to the car to get it. Just as he was about to do just that, they arrived at their destination. He did a quick scan of the area, but didn't notice anything amiss. He allowed himself to relax just a little bit.

"There's a portable building we can go chill in. It's right over here." She walked off. Corey could see the portable buildings lined up. Maybe 60 yards away. He allowed her to lead him there.

"They don't keep it locked up?" he asked.

"Yeah. But it ain't shit to pick the locks," she admitted. She reached in her purse, pulled out a bobby pin and began to fiddle with the lock. Corey just stood there, watching out.

Seconds later, she opened the door. They both walked in. "Damn, it's dark as fuck in here," he told her. The room was totally devoid of light. As if someone had boarded up the windows. He waited for her response. It never came.

Instead, he felt the metal of a gun barrel pressed against the back of his head. "Don't do nothing stupid, nigga. Get on your knees."

"Look, dawg. You can have whatever, but I ain't getting on my knees. Just tell . . ." *Thwack!* The gunman smacked the pistol against the back of Corey's skull. He stumbled and fell into a desk. "Agghh," he groaned, as he lay on the floor bleeding, his head pounding, feeling like his brain was swelling in his head.

The light switch flipped. The whole room became illuminated. Standing over him, with a .45 pointed at him, was a 6'4", 230 lbs. dark-skinned nigga with a gapped tooth. He watched Corey, as ole girl made her final exit out the door.

Corey shook his head. He couldn't believe it. He let some country bumpkins get the drop and run a play on him. His head was pounding so much, he couldn't even think straight. "Empty out your pockets, nigga," Black dude growled. "And take that shit off and throw it over here."

Dying over something you could get back was stupid as hell to Corey. His main objective was to make it out alive. Afterwards, he'd worry about getting his lick back.

He reached into his pocket and pulled his knot out. It was his entire savings. What was left from what he brought with him. *A little over six bands.* He removed his Cuban link, as well as his bracelet. His watch was the last thing to come off. He chunked everything at the dude's feet.

Dude scooped everything up, placing it all in a Crown Royal bag. "Bitch ass nigga," he sneered. "You thought you was gonna fuck my lil sister, huh? I bet you one of those soft ass niggas. If we was in the pen and you was my celly, I'd fuck you, boy." *What the fuck?*

Corey tried to make sense of the shit. Now, dude on some straight up out-the-pen type of time? *Ain't no stupid shit!* Corey was definitely not about to go for that. His eyes quickly darted around, searching for any type of weapon.

Sure enough, the big black nigga started fumbling with his belt buckle. "Yeah. That's what Imma do. Since you wanna try and fuck my lil sister. Imma fuck you. Maybe, I might just make you suck my dick. Like a good lil bitch."

Corey's adrenaline had his body trembling. He didn't give a fuck if he had to die to protect his manhood. He told himself, if dude's dick gets anywhere near his face, that motherfucker's coming off. He wasn't about to let *no* nigga violate him.

Something caught his eye. The door to the portable building crept open. Someone stepped inside. Corey couldn't see anything but the person's shoes. A pair of *Cool Gray's.* The same kind Happy wore to the party.

Corey's heart leapt for joy. He didn't want to tip the dude off, so he made it a point to stare him in his eyes. Just as he reached into his boxers to pull his dick out, *'Thwack!'* Happy smacked him across his head with the butt of the gun, with enough force behind it to knock dude smooth out. He collapsed, face first. Asleep!

Happy looked down on Corey with a magnanimous smile. "Damn, nigga, I can't leave your ass alone for a second, huh?" Corey hopped onto his feet, snatched the Crown Royal bag with all his belongings. Before he could second guess himself, he snatched Happy's pistol out his hand, aimed it at the back of dude's head and fired three shots. *Bocka. Bocka. Bocka.*

His skull opened up like a busted cantaloupe. Skull and brain bits splattered over Happy and Corey's shoes. "Pussy ass nigga!" Corey screamed, still visibly shaken. "Suck on that, bitch boy!" He kicked him for good measure.

The two of them made a quick dash out, not wanting to draw attention, but needing to get somewhere else quickly. They sped walked all the way to Happy's car, afraid to say one word, until they were safely heading back home.

"What the fuck, Kinfolk. Who the hell was that?" Corey finally asked, once his nerve returned.

"That was a nigga named Pig. He just came home about two months ago," Happy informed him.

"Mannnn. Dude was in that bitch trynna violate a nigga," Corey said, still not believing he almost got raped. "Well, he would have lost his life long before that happened."

"I can believe it. They say dude was in the pen fucking with them boys. Supposedly he'd checked in to Protective Custody, just so he could play in that mud. I guess all those rumors were facts," Happy said, shaking his head in disgust.

Corey realized something. "How you knew where I was at?"

"I came back from fucking that bitch Deedra. I couldn't find you, so I asked around. Even though they didn't know your name, when I described what you had on, Deedra's home girl, Brittney, said you left the party with that hoe Barbie. I already knew what the bidness was."

"So what . . . that bitch be on some set up shit?" Corey asked, perturbed.

"Yeah. They don't fuck with nobody from round here though. They must have thought you were there by yourself. If they would've known you were with me, they wouldn't have tried you," Happy admitted.

"That's another thing, bruh, why you left a nigga? You know I don't know none of these fucking people!"

"My bad, Kinfolk. That hoe Deedra a fool on that dick, plus she got that snap back. But you right, I shouldn't have left you." Happy agreed.

Corey's anger dissipated some. "Oh. Here." He handed Happy back his strap.

"Damn, boy. You opened that nigga shit up. I wish you would have told me something." Happy grimaced as they pulled back up to the house. "Look, bruh, don't say shit around Tee Tee. If she asks, we were at the trap grinding all night."

"I got you, Kinfolk. Your secrets are *always* safe with me." They shook and dabbed each other up, before heading inside to face the lady of the house.

As they walked in, Tee Tee was up, dressed in a yellow robe, waiting for Happy in the living room. Corey couldn't help but wonder what she had on underneath. Her face was set in a scowl. Her arms folded across her ample breast. "Nigga. Where the fuck have you been?" She seethed.

"We were at the trap, Tee. Don't start your shit, girl," Happy claimed, exasperatedly.

"At the trap, huh? Okay, well, tell me why that stank ass thot Deedra posted all on the Gram, talking 'bout she saw *her boo Happy* at that party Lil Tay threw last night?"

"Shit. I don't know. You know these hoes be capping on the Gram just to piss your nutty ass off. And you fall for that shit every time. If you don't believe me, ask my cousin Corey."

She turned around and mugged Corey. He wasn't sure how much weight his word would hold. She had to know he wouldn't tell on Happy, no matter what. "Yeah, Tee Tee. We were at the trap all night. I even asked Happy if he knew any females he could put me down with. He told me naw, because you gon' be tripping," Corey finessed. The way he said it gave her the impression her behavior was proof Happy was right.

She gave him a look, like she didn't believe a word he said. But, the mission was already completed. Corey distracted her long enough so Happy could jump in the shower. She must have realized her mistake. As soon as she heard the shower running, her head snapped around. "Oh, naw, naw, nigga. Why your ass go hop straight in the shower? You know Imma wanna smell your dick," Tee Tee called out, disappearing into the bedroom.

Corey shook his head and chuckled at the couple. He stripped down to his shorts, and got comfortable on the couch. He really wanted to slide up in something wet and warm. Even though the bitch Barbie had set him up, he *still* wanted to put the dick on her. Now, more than ever. Fuck her, until she begs for him to stop. Then, he would dig in and fuck her even harder.

Suddenly, for some reason, he started thinking about Tee Tee. About how fat and juicy her pussy looked, when she was bending over in the fridge that day. His balls began to ache. His body temperature began rising. He gripped his hardened cock and stroked himself feverishly. He closed his eyes and pictured Tee's juicy booty wobbling, as he hit her from the back. Just as his nut popped and cracked, he heard a gasp.

"Oh shit!" His eyes shot open. Tee was standing behind the couch, eyes wide, jaw dropped. Once he saw her, she tried to avert her eyes. "My bad, Corey. I didn't mean . . . I was on my way to the . . . I didn't . . . Fuck!" She kept stammering and stuttering.

Corey was stuck. With cum all over his hands, he couldn't do much but apologize as he tried to get up to go clean himself. "Uhh. Can you get me a napkin," he asked, bashfully.

"Oh. Yeah, yeah, I got you." Tee Tee rushed to the kitchen, grabbed a napkin and brought it to him. As she handed it to him, her eyes traveled from his dick to his cum-coated hand. She subconsciously wet her bottom lip.

Corey grabbed his dick and wiped the nut off, making sure to squeeze until the rest of it bubbled to the surface. Tee Tee just stood there. Transfixed. Hypnotized.

He looked up at her, letting his dick fall. Nothing was said. Just two adults staring intensely at one another. Suddenly, Tee Tee snapped and came back to her senses. With a mumbled apology, she shuffled back into her room.

Corey didn't know what to think or do. On one hand, he knew it was some slime ball shit to be lusting after his cousin's woman. A cousin that welcomed him into his home. Even after he found out what type of problems Corey was running from.

On the other hand, Tee Tee was fine as fuck. And Corey was just a man. A man with a hard dick, who hadn't gotten it wet in a while. He didn't know how long he would live without a wet coochie to slide into, but from the look Tee Tee gave him, it wouldn't be long before Corey was balls deep in his cousin's girlfriend.

As he laid back down and prepared to go to bed, he heard the unmistakable sound of lips smacking and skin slapping. Hot and steamy sex.

It seemed like Corey wasn't the only one worked up after the encounter. He stayed awake listening to Tee Tee take dick like a champ. Corey might have been tripping, but it seemed like she was louder than usual. Wonder why?

Club Heat was packed from the front to the back. It was Wednesday night, so it was grown and sexy. *Twenty-one and up.* Laura was on the prowl. Dressed in a form-fitting, black and white Cavalli dress. She accentuated it with a pair of cocaine-white Botega heels. With no bra, her titties sat up perfectly. Courtesy of her boob job.

Even though she was forty plus, Laura loved her a young nigga. Nothing felt better than having a young nigga ride her hard and fast. She appreciated making love, but she *loved* getting fucked. And the young ones were always quick to deliver just that.

She waltzed in and headed straight to the bar. "Give me two shots of Patron," she told the cute, brown-skinned bartender. "What's your name, honey?" she purred.

"Austin."

"Austin? Okay, Austin, do you have a girlfriend?"

"Umm. As a matter of fact, I do," he reluctantly said.

"Ahh. Well, that's too bad. I might have wanted to take you home for the night. But, I don't want you to get in any trouble."

Austin blushed. "Here you go."

"Laura, honey. My name is Laura. If you're ever tired of your girlfriend and want a *woman* friend, don't hesitate to give me a call." Laura slid him her card, and grabbed her two shot glasses. He nodded, pocketed the card, then moved to the next customer.

She downed both shots in quick succession. The liquor burned through her chest. Her clit began to pulsate. She rubbed her thighs together. Now, she was glad she decided to wear panties. Tonight was going to be one of those nights. She would definitely need a juice catcher.

Laura sat at the bar and scanned the club. There were a lot of sexy people in the building. She spotted a light-skinned woman in a pink and white Fendi dress, with a pair of white suede, knee-high Fendi boots. *She's definitely killing it,* Laura thought to herself. She was intrigued.

The woman was in VIP, surrounded by mostly men and a few women. Laura wondered. She turned around and ordered two more shots of Patron. After her second double shot, Laura felt no pain. The intrigue was too much to bear.

She got up and made her way over to the VIP. The closer she got, the more she realized that the woman was responsible for her panties flooding. Laura wouldn't really consider herself bisexual. Though, she did "experiment" quite a few times. It takes a special type of woman to make her kitty purr.

Laura stood right outside the velvet ropes that sectioned off the VIP. Buzzed and extremely horny, she bit her lip. Meme locked eyes with her immediately. She recognized Laura's lust. Her hunger. Her wanton need.

Meme had been dancing with a bottle of Rosé held high in her hand. She walked over to where Laura stood. "You thirsty?"

"All the time," Laura replied seductively.

"Open up." Laura tilted her head back. Meme turned the bottle upside down, pouring expensive champagne down her throat. After Laura successfully swallowed, Meme removed the rope and allowed her entry into her kingdom.

The two women introduced themselves, then spent the rest of the night partying. Like it was the end of the world.

Three hours later, Laura was on her back with her legs wide open. A twenty-two-year-old dark-skinned nigga knelt next to her head, feeding her his hot and heavy dick. Laura's left hand gripped him, forcing him to go deeper down her throat. Her right hand fondled his nuts.

Between her thighs, Meme sucked greedily on her pussy while another bright skinned twenty-four-year-old street nigga gutted her out from the back.

After the club, the two women decided to continue the party. Snatching up two young men out of VIP, they brought them both to the room. Planning some X-rated cougar fun. The rest of the night was spent with two veteran women, showing them young cubs how it's done.

Chapter 11

It was raining, and it had been doing so for the last hour. Ty sat in her car, patiently watching. Waiting. Still no sign of the treacherous bitch, Meme. After Ty discovered her baby boy was executed and thrown away like trash, she made a decision. The rest of the time she had left on Earth, she would use it to make everyone that's responsible suffer. And first on her list? Her former best friend.

Ty had been parked in Meme's apartments since 7 a.m. It was going on 6 p.m. Meme had yet to show her face. Ty paid one of the block boys one hundred dollars to go knock on the door. That's how she knew she wasn't home.

She fingered the trigger on her compact Glock 9 she purchased just for this occasion. The hatred she harbored burned bright in her soul. There was no more room for kindness or forgiveness. Revenge consumed her completely, her patience wearing thin.

Ty cranked the car up, ready to call it quits for the day. Suddenly, she saw a late model Ford sedan pull up and drop somebody off. She watched intensely, praying it was Meme. Instead, it was Meme's estranged boyfriend, Slick.

Slick recently bonded out of jail for the altercation with Meme. And, he was not too happy about it. Not only did she pull some fuck shit by calling the laws, but she also refused to answer the phone.

He had to call his grandparents to bond him out. Now, he was on his way back to the apartment. Even though the courts told him he had to stay clear of her, Slick needed to grab his things. He just hoped she wouldn't be home.

As he unlocked the door and walked into the apartment, Slick noticed the place looked exactly the same as the day he went to jail. Well, except for the fact that Meme cleaned up a little. He carefully searched the one-bedroom apartment for any signs of life.

Slick could tell, Meme hadn't been there for a while. *What the fuck?* He wondered where she could be. *Did she move in with another nigga?* was the first thing his mind went to. He grabbed some trash bags and started filling them up with his stuff. His shoes, his clothes and whatever else he could find that belonged to him. *Knock! Knock! Knock!*

Who the fuck could that be? Slick wondered, as he made his way to go answer it. He opened the door and was surprised to see Meme's best friend, Ty, standing on the doorstep, soaking wet. "She ain't here," he said, assuming Ty was there looking for Meme.

"I know. Can I come in until the rain stops? I ain't trynna walk back to the car through this shit," Ty asked. The rain had picked up tremendously. Now it was pouring down cats and dogs.

Slick didn't even think twice about it. He stepped to the side and allowed her entry. He gave her a once-over. Ty was rocking a navy blue hoodie, blue jeans and some blue and white sketchers. She looked drenched. "You need a towel?" he offered.

"Yeah. Thank you."

He went to retrieve one. By the time he returned, Ty ditched the hoodie as well as the blue jeans. She sat in the living room in a T-shirt, a pair of small purple panties and her Rugrat socks. "Whoah!" Slick stutter stepped. He'd never seen Ty like that before.

He tried to avert his eyes as he handed her the towel. She grabbed it and said, "Boy, stop that. We're practically like family. I need to dry my shit. Do you have a blow dryer?"

"Uhh. Yeah. I'm pretty sure Meme has one," he told her, as he scurried off to find it. *Damn, she got a fat ass pussy,* he thought to himself, as he grabbed the blow dryer.

After handing it over, it was next to impossible for Slick to just go back to packing. So instead, he stayed in the living room to see what Ty had going on. She plugged the dryer up and sat her clothes on the recliner.

As she blow-dried, she asked," So, what's Meme been up to?"

Slick really didn't want to tell her about the falling out he had with Meme. "Shit, she's been . . . Well, you know . . . Meme," he replied vaguely. Ty shuffled her feet as she continued to blow dry.

He couldn't help but stare at her ass, as she leaned over. Her purple panties looked a little too snug on her. They kept digging in her crevices every time she moved. Her coochie lips hung out the sides of the crotch band.

It was hard to think about anything else, but the sight before him. "What time do you think she'll be back?" Ty asked over her shoulder. It wasn't lost on her how Slick couldn't keep his eyes off her fat ass. Matter of fact, she counted on that. "Slick?"

"Huh?" He finally responded.

"Do you know what time she'll be back?"

"Umm. Naw, I don't. To be honest with you, Ty, I don't know where she's at. Your guess is as good as mine. She hasn't even been answering her phone for me." The last thing Slick wanted to do was talk about Meme, especially when he had Ty in his living room. Practically naked. All he could think about was bussing her ass up.

"Is that why you're looking at me like that?" Ty asked, mischief dripping off her words.

"Like what?" Slick didn't think it was that obvious.

"Like you wanna see if this fat ass pussy is as good as it looks," Ty said, boldly.

His dick twitched at the remark. Ty was turning him on, something fierce. *Maybe I should fuck Meme's best friend. Why not? She sent me to jail, and left me there to rot.* "I ain't gonna lie,

Ty, a nigga definitely feeling your vibe right now. And that cat *do* look scrumptious," he complimented.

Ty set the blow dryer down, then turned around. "Oh yeah? Well, let me see what you're working with. Maybe we can make something happen."

Slick didn't waste any time. He quickly unbuttoned his jeans and yanked them off. Then came his boxers. Slick sat on the couch bare ass. Nothing on, but a black Rocawear shirt.

Ty stared at his piece. "Okay. You might be working with something." She already knew Slick had a nice sized dick, and that he knew how to use it. Meme would often say that was the only reason she kept him around. But, at that moment, it wasn't about pleasure. It was about something else.

She slinked towards Slick, then dropped to her knees. Ty gripped him with her left hand. His dick became ridged in her fist. "Ssshit, Ty," Slick moaned, as she jacked him off.

"Damn, boy. You got a big ass dick," she purred as she stroked him in earnest.

"Don't play with it. Let a nigga feel the back of your throat," Slick urged, fiending to feel something wet around his cock.

"Relax, baby. Momma gon' give you exactly what you need." Slick did just that. He leaned his head back against the couch and closed his eyes.

Suddenly, Ty released her grip on his dick. He opened his eyes and looked down at her. He found himself, staring down the barrel of a gun. Before he could open his mouth to say a word, '*Bocka*'.

Slick's head snapped back, bouncing off the back of the couch. His body ricocheted, then fell to the right. His forehead crushed in. The back of his head was a hole the size of a quarter.

Ty just stared, unblinking, her face was pepper-sprayed with blood. Bits of Slick's cranium, littered her hair. Her skin felt greasy and slick. No pun intended. Without the slightest remorse, Ty stood up and headed to the kitchen sink to wash her hair, face and hands. After she finished drying her clothes, she walked smoothly out of the apartment. As if she didn't have a care in the world.

Three hours later, Meme finally decided to stop by her apartment. She needed to grab a few of her things. Since she'd hit that lick on Ty, she'd only been by her spot a few times. Each time, just to grab a few items.

Meme had relocated. She paid for six months in advance on a condo in midtown. Also, she dropped ten thousand down on a new Jaguar XF. She knew Ty would eventually come looking for her. She'd be damned if she got caught laying up in the same spot she'd been in.

As she turned into her apartments, police were scattered everywhere. Meme really didn't think too much of it. Twice a month, it was guaranteed. A dead body would pop up somewhere in the apartments. But, as she got closer to her spot, an eerie feeling began to take hold of her. One of the block boys was standing outside.

She rolled her window down, and called him over. "Say, Brick. What's going on?"

Brick looked surprised to see her. He didn't recognize the car. "I don't know, you tell me. They talkin 'bout a dead body's in *your* shit."

"What?" Meme's eyes became big as quarters.

"Yeah. At first, I thought it was you. But, they say it's some nigga. Twelve ain't brought the body out yet. That's what everybody's waiting for. Your neighbor Ms. Whitmore says she thinks it's your nigga. What was his name?" Brick tried to recollect.

"Slick?" Meme asked, feeling herself about to puke.

"Yeah, yeah. That's his name. She thinks it's him," Brick confirmed.

Meme couldn't believe it. Slick got out of jail. And might be dead in her apartment? She wanted to stay and get more answers. But, the last thing she needed was the cops getting all in her mix.

"A'ight, Brick, I'm 'bout to bounce. Do me a favor. Don't tell *nobody* you saw me. And when they pull the body out, hit me and let me know who it is." Meme made sure Brick still had her phone number.

"For shit sho," he replied. Meme rolled her window up and got the hell out of dodge. Her mind raced, as she made her way back to her condo. She didn't know what the hell was going on, but she had a suspicion it was due to what she had done.

Not only did she help Pat kidnap little CJ, but she turned around and stole the ransom money from Ty. Preventing her from getting her son back. When Meme found out Pat actually killed CJ and discarded his body in a dumpster, she was smart enough to know she needed to get somewhere. She was a loose end in his eyes. Just like J Wright and Carleen. Both of them were already dead.

Meme thought about leaving the state. She had no way of knowing if Pat killed Slick, or if Ty sent her young goon Marcus to do it. There was no doubt in her mind, it had to be one of them. Either way, she was going to have to lay low for a while.

As she left the East, hopped on I-10 headed West, her eyes kept darting back and forth in her rearview. Dread consumed her. She didn't know what to do. Wait. That was a lie. She did know what to do. *Stay alive!*

Marcus and Chief had been combing the streets for days. So far, they hadn't picked up on any leads. Either dudes didn't know shit, or they were extremely tight lipped. It wasn't as if they weren't applying any pressure. Damn near every person they questioned left with a broken body part.

They saw a group of people standing out at the car wash on Wallisville. *Why not?* They decided to try their luck, and turned in. Many, or the ones out there, were young niggas. A few old-schools and the smoker named Le Le.

Marcus pulled up, hopped out with his Sig tucked into his hoodie's pocket. The first person he approached was a young trapper by the name of Lil Harvey. Harvey had just made nineteen two days ago. He was still high off celebrating.

"Say. Look out, lil homie, let me holla at you for a second." Harvey didn't like the vibe Marcus was giving off. He noticed how Chief was mugging and felt it might be wiser to see what they had to say first. Plus, he'd left his pole under the seat of his box Chevy Caprice.

Harvey walked over to them. Marcus began. "Say . . . Have you heard anything 'bout the lil boy they found in the dumpster a couple weeks ago?"

"Shit. Who hasn't. That's some straight up foul shit. Niggas think it's gangsta to kill defenseless lil kids these days. You don't get no stripes for that!" Harvey spat with disgust.

Marcus and Chief nodded in agreement. "You ain't heard anything about who might have done it?" Harvey took a step back, giving Marcus and Chief a questioning look. Chief recognized, and figured he knew the cause.

"Look, my nigga. We ain't trynna put *Twelve* on nobody's trail. The lil nigga was like a son to my bro here," Chief clarified.

Harvey looked at Marcus with a new set of eyes. "Naw, my nigga. I wish I did. What's your info? If I do, I'll pull up on you. My lil nephew and the lil homie are the same age," he confided.

While shaking his head, Marcus exchanged contact information. He was about to hop into the whip, when Le Le approached. "Say, look out, young blood. Lemme holla at you for a sec."

Marcus looked at Chief, both wondering, what could this old, dingy ass dope fiend want. "Wassup, school?" Le Le smelled so bad, Marcus had to hold his breath while he talked to him.

"I heard you talking 'bout that lil boy they found in the trash bin a few weeks back." That got Marcus's full attention.

"Yeah. Why? You hear something?" Le Le began to fidget. Now that Marcus and Chief had their unwavering gaze on him, he wasn't so sure this was a good idea.

"Uhh. Well, yeah. Okay, so my lady friend Carleen and I were getting high one day. She up and told me she was supposed to be coming into some money. Something about having a lil boy at her house. She said, after one week, she would get a thousand dollars. Well, a week went by. They found that lil boy in a trash bin and Carleen in the trunk of that no good nigga, J Wright's car."

Marcus's heart started to gallop. His chest tightened. This was their first solid lead. "Do you know who hired them? The person who was gonna pay the money?"

Le Le looked around nervously. As if the person he was thinking of might pop up out of the bushes at any time. He nodded. His eyes kept darting back and forth, between Marcus and Chief.

"Who, skool?" Marcus pressed.

"Pat Pat."

That piece of news hit Marcus like a ton of bricks. Now, it all made sense. He thought he would have felt better once he found out who was behind everything. But now, he felt worse. Why? Because he was the catalyst.

He was the one that robbed Pat. *He must have somehow thought Ty had something to do with it. But how did he know I even fuck with Ty,* Marcus thought. He stood there, stunned. Speechless.

Chief went in his pocket and gave Le Le a $20 bill. "Go grab you a shot, skool." Le Le skipped off. Happier than a punk in a dick factory. Chief and Marcus hopped back in the car, and just sat there.

Marcus felt like shit. How could he tell Ty the reason CJ had gotten kidnapped was because of him. Would she ever forgive him? *Of course not!* He decided right then, he wouldn't tell her. This was something he would take to the grave. What he will tell her, though, is he found out Pat was behind it. As long as she knew who to go after, she didn't need Pat's reasoning for doing what they did.

One thing for sure, Marcus wouldn't stop until the pain was paid back in full. He was so lost in his thoughts, he didn't hear Chief blurt out, "Oh, shit! That's crazy than a bitch!" He stared at Marcus, grinning wickedly.

"What the fuck is you grinning 'bout?" Marcus asked, slightly annoyed.

"Mannn. I just thought about something. That nigga Mya fucks with, Jeremiah, that's Pat's nephew."

"Hold up. Wait. Say what? You sure?" Marcus couldn't believe their luck.

"Facts. I went to school with the nigga. He plays football. His uncle threw him a big ass birthday bash over the summer. Copped him a new whip and everything." The last part was said with a hint of jealousy.

Evil thoughts lurked behind Marcus's eyebrows. "We can snatch the nigga Jeremiah up and wait on Pat to make a move." Then, common sense struck him in the face. "Wait. I can't do that, my nigga. Mya's in love with that fool. She would never forgive me."

"Okay. Well then, I'll do it," Chief offered. "If you want, I won't even tell you were I keep the nigga at. That way, you don't have to worry 'bout lying to her."

Marcus slowly nodded, warming up to that idea. "Bet that." They pulled up to the house. All the lights were off. Ty was sitting in the dark. "Ty. Ty. Baby!" Marcus grabbed her by her shoulders, shaking her back to her senses.

She slowly looked at him, as if coming out of a hypnotic state. Marcus waited until they locked eyes with each other. "We found out who, baby. We finally found out who did this!" he said excitedly.

Ty's eyes sparkled. Before she could fix her lips to ask who, Marcus blurted out: "Pat Pat." She slunk back, as if she got hit with a back-handed slap. He saw the skepticism on her face. He went on to tell her everything he'd learned. Then, it hit her. *The restaurant!*

The restaurant they found the body at was the same one Pat took her to, when they first went out. Ty knew then, without a shadow of a doubt, it was Pat. Her skepticism turned to certainty. Then the certainty turned to rage. She *needed* to kill something.

Meme would have to wait, for now. Pat had bumped up to the main course. "We might have a way to get at that nigga." Marcus told her about Jeremiah being Pat's nephew. "We can't tell Mya," he said, with sadness in his eyes.

"I agree," Ty replied. Her, Marcus and Chief, sat in the living room and put their plan together. They'd been on defense the whole time. Now, it was time for the triangle offense.

Sticking to the plan, Marcus and Ty stayed at home with Mya. Meanwhile, Chief hunted her boyfriend down. It took two hours of stalking before Chief found an opportunity to knock him out, then stick him in the trunk of the car.

Now, he had the boy tied and stuffed in the closet like a pair of sneakers. Even though Marcus agreed Chief wouldn't disclose the location of where he was keeping Jeremiah, Ty wasn't trying to hear none of that. She wanted the first crack at cracking Jeremiah.

Ty pulled up to the location. She honestly didn't know what she would do. She just felt the overwhelming need to hurt someone, and Pat's nephew would have to do.

As she walked into the dilapidated and vermin-infested vacant home, Ty felt exhilarated. Chief met her in the living room. "Where's he at?" She deadpanned.

"Bedroom closet." Chief led her towards the back of the house. Jeremiah was tied up, withering in fear. Chief duct-taped his eyes shut and his mouth closed.

Ty knelt down and peeled the tape over his mouth back. "Jeremiah, do you know who this is?" she asked coldly.

Jeremiah cocked his head to the side, trying his best to register, then recognized. "Mya's mom?" he asked, confused and unsure. He felt he had to be mistaken. Why would Mya's mom be mixed up in all this? Surely, his ears were playing tricks on him.

"Yes, this is me, Jeremiah. Before you ask . . . No. Mya doesn't know anything about this. And, if you cooperate, it would be *your* decision to tell her. Once all this gets sorted out. But first, I need some answers. As you know, my son was taken from me. What you may have not known, your uncle was the one responsible."

Recognition, confusion, then fear, manifested itself on Jeremiah's face. Ty studied his reaction. She could tell that he didn't know. Still, none of that mattered. At the end of the day, anyone related to Pat was fair game.

"Ms. T. I don't know what's going on, or what my uncle did. You have to believe me. I love Mya too much to do anything to hurt her, or her family." Ty watched Jeremiah dispassionately, as he tried his best to convince her.

Once she grew tired of listening, she rose up and whispered something to Chief. "Find out where his bitch ass Uncle's at. Then. Get rid of him." Chief nodded. Ty walked back through the house and out the front door.

If she would have detected any falseness on Jeremiah, she would have made him suffer. His only crime was being born to a polluted bloodline. Be that as it may, she needed answers, and Ty elected Chief to be the one to get them for her. For the rest of the night, Chief went to work on Jeremiah, trying to squeeze every drop of info out of him.

It had been 43 days since Bo caught the case that sent him to closed custody. Him and his celly, Time Bomb, had gotten real close. They sparred, worked out, and played chess. Constantly.

Bo ended up opening up to Bomb. About his situation and how he ended up messing with punks. After hearing how Brown Sugar was paying for Bo's appeal attorney, Bomb wasn't too sure he wouldn't have played that same role. *"I ain't never do nothing sexual with dude,"* Bo claimed one night.

As they sat up playing chess, the officer on duty dropped off a lay in on Bo's bunk. He grabbed it and read: *U.C.C. Committee.* "Celly. They done overturned you case," Time Bomb suggested.

"You think so. I didn't get any notice in the mail asking for an extension," Bo said, as he contemplated what this could mean. If he went back to population, how would it be? Truthfully, he was cool with being back there on G-5.

He wasn't a fool. He knew the only reason the Blood's on G-5 ain't come for him was because of Bomb. Population was a different story. He wasn't a hoe. He had proven that, many times. Still, he was solo. So, that meant he was one deep, in a sea of sharks. Bo made sure he got some rest, to go see U.C.C. the next morning.

It turned out, it *was* a reversal. Due to the fuck up on the part of one the ranking officers who administered aid to the response, plus the paper work of a 20-year writ writer, Bo was headed back to population.

As he walked down the hallways he noticed all the staring, whispers, and head nods. His move slip said he was headed back to his old block.

While he was in G-5, it was rumored that Rose was messing with Double R now. When he used to shoot Rose kites, he would never get any back. To be honest, he wasn't even that upset. It was bad enough he had Brown Sugar coming to see him, but to be living with a flaming homosexual? That was way too much.

He arrived on J Block. Dudes acted as if they'd seen a ghost. Some walked up on him, gave him dap. Congratulations on overturning his case. Others stayed their distance. They didn't like Bo doing what he did. They felt he had no right to get upset about someone exposing him. If he was a real nigga like he claimed, he would let the world know.

What if he had given the female officer something sexually transmittable. That's how they looked at it. But, even though they felt some type of way, they whispered instead of approaching. Many had seen Bo in action. They knew he was certified from the shoulders. No one on the whole ranch wanted to fuck with him. At least not head up.

As he prepared to go into his new cell, he had to walk by his old one. He couldn't resist. As he walked by, he glanced inside. Double R was sitting on the sink. Rose was sitting on the bed. They were engrossed in a conversation.

Double R saw Bo, and jumped in shock. He didn't know what type of timing Bo would be on. In his mind, Bo was in love with Rose. Or, at least that's what Rose claimed. Rose noticed the shocked look on Double R's face, turned his head and *his* jaw dropped. "Bo . . . Uh . . .Hey," Rose stammered. Bo just looked at them both, shook his head and kept walking towards his cell.

His celly was a white dude named Shadow. As soon as he walked in, Bo noticed it was going to be a problem. The cell was dusty. The sockets were burnt to a crisp. Shadow was sitting on the toilet, sleeping, with his head in his lap. A long line of drool was hanging from his lip. The cell smelled of smoke. *A Toon (K-2) Head!* Bo thought as he sat his property down.

He was a firm believer in: *how you do your time is your business.* But, when your time starts impeding on his, then there's a problem. He waited until his celly's high dissipated and he shook him all the way back. Then, Bo laid down the ground rules.

"First things first, you 'bout to clean this cell up," Bo told him. Shadow wasn't a fighter by no means; he just wanted to get high. Everyone knew about Bo's hands, so when Bo gave the order to clean, Shadow wasted no time getting to it.

Bo hopped on his bunk, to give his celly enough room to do what needed to be done. Shadow went about scrubbing the cell, wall to wall. Top to bottom. Bo wasn't a bully, but at the same time, he definitely wasn't a hoe. He, for damn sure, wasn't about to be cleaning up after no grown ass man. As if he was his bitch or something.

After he felt like the cell was clean enough, Bo began to get adjusted. He went to the day room for a few hours. Just to give *whoever* ample opportunity to speak their peace.

He told Shadow, *"You can smoke, as long as I'm not in the cell. But whatever they find in this bitch, belongs to you. Understood?"* Shadow nodded. *"And make sure you clean up after yourself. I don't want to see no doobies."* Bo left him to his own devices.

The day room was packed. Bo sat in front of the sports TV, watching highlights. The Mavericks played the Timberwolves. He waited to see if Rose and Double R would come out. They didn't. On the last in and out, he went up to tell Shadow he needed some cell time.

As he walked by Rose's cell, he noticed the sheet was up. Double R was standing at the bars. Rose was behind the sheet. He already knew what time it was. He mugged Double R, but didn't say anything.

Once Bo got in the cell, he bird-bathed, fixed something to eat, then read until he fell asleep. Showers were in the morning. He wasn't about to miss it.

At 5:30 a.m., the officer on the block yelled "shower time." Bo hopped up, hit his grill real quick, grabbed his shower gear, and made his way down the hallway.

As soon as he entered the shower area, he couldn't see a foot in front of him. The showers were misty as hell. It looked like thick, white smoke everywhere. He quickly found his usual shower head, close to the back and began washing his ass.

It never occurred to him, being in the back was a dangerous place to be. As he was soaping up, he felt someone creep up from behind him. Before he could turn around to assess the threat, they grabbed his face, yanking it backwards. Simultaneously, Bo felt a blinding, sharp pain, biting at his lower back. He grunted, as he felt the cold metal penetrate his skin.

He tried to fight his assailant off. The wet surface, accompanied by his fleeing strength, wouldn't allow it. Whoever had a grip on him was just too strong. Bo fought with all the strength he had left. It was no use. So while he was naked and helpless in the shower, Bo was repeatedly stabbed. Left to bleed to death, on the nasty, filthy bathroom floor.

The pain was so excruciating. His muscles spasmed and jerked. His teeth chattered. A horrible chill traveled through his body. As he lay on the ground bleeding out, the last thing he remembered was someone yelling out "Medical!" His eyelids seemed to close on their own.

Chapter 12

Corey, Happy and one of Happy's homeboys named Keeno, were posted up in the trap. Happy had been pushing hard and soft for years. He'd recently gotten ahold of some new shit called Demon Dust. He began to push a little here and a little there. Just to see what the fiends were saying.

His customers loved it. He planned on making a very big purchase soon. Keeno was pushing K-2. A lot of the new age smokers were mixing the crack and the K-2 together. All in all, the trap was booming, and it was only 1:30 p.m.

Since Corey really didn't have any drugs to move yet, Happy tossed him a couple hundred, just to hold the fort down. He sat in front of the monitor all day, Draco clutched and fully loaded. He would let his mind drift from time to time.

Images of Tee Tee clouded his thoughts. He didn't know what the fuck was wrong with him. Happy was keeping it all the way "G", and here he was fantasizing about fucking his girl. Corey knew it was wrong as fuck, but he couldn't help it.

Since he'd been in Cleveland, he still hadn't gotten his dick wet. It's not that there wasn't a steady supply of women to choose from, but when you're on the possible run for a double homicide, you don't tend to get out much to meet them. Then, ever since the situation with Barbie, he'd been really reluctant to jump out there with another female he didn't know.

So instead, he just focused on trying to get his bread back up. He only had a couple bands left, and soon he would be broke. He couldn't have that. Corey had to admit it, the trap Happy had, rolled harder than anything he ever saw in the city.

Since they'd pulled up at 8:45 a.m., Corey estimated at least seventy licks had come through in four and a half hours. "Damn. We done ran out of wraps. Say, Corey, you feel like making a run real quick?" Happy asked, as he stood in front of the microwave. Staring intensely. Babysitting a pot that was in the oven.

"A'ight. I ain't tripping. What y'all need?"

"Grab me some wraps, some Flaming Hots, and a strawberry Fanta," Happy ordered.

Keeno thought for a second. "Fuck with me on a big bag of Funions. Oh, and a Sprite Remix." They both each gave Corey a ten-dollar bill. He grabbed the keys to Happy's candy blue "El Dog", and made his way to the store.

On the way there, he saw a smoker walking down the street that he recognized. She had just left the trap a half hour ago. She had on a light pink and white sundress, with some flats. Corey noticed her body when she came to cop the fifty slab. She was thick as hell. Brown-skinned. Her titties sagged a bit. But considering she looked to be in her mid-forties, you couldn't hold that against her.

He couldn't remember what name Happy called her, but he doubted she was a set up chick. He pulled up beside her. "Hey, skool. You need a ride?"

She looked at him. Her face had a light sheen of sweat, despite the chill in the air. Corey got a closer look at her. She was still beautiful. She couldn't have been smoking long. "You don't even know where I'm headed. What if I need a ride to California," she joked.

"I'd say, we need to stop for gas." Corey got a smile out of that. "But honestly, I figured you stayed somewhere close in town. I doubt a beautiful woman like you would be walking far." She smiled even brighter, while reaching for the door handle. "I'm Corey," he greeted.

"I'm Sandra. Nice to meet you." Corey pulled off.

Ten minutes later, he had the "El Dog" parked a few houses down from the house Sandra and her husband, Eddie, shared. His seat leaned all the way back, while she gobbled his cock with passion and precision. It didn't take long for Corey to proposition her with fifty dollars for a blowjob. The way she saw it, he just paid for her dope.

She told him: Since her husband expected her to be walking, she had a good ten to fifteen minutes before she was due home. Plenty of time to bust one down her throat.

With his hand gripping her weave in his fist, Corey slammed her head onto his dick. *'Awka. Awka. Awka.'* Sandra choked, as Corey took out his sexual frustration on the back of her throat. His toes curled in his Lebron's. His balls began to boil. Sweat pooled between his ass cheeks. Sandra took the abuse and hungered for more. She opened her throat all the way up.

Corey's balls tapped against her chin, as she deep-throated a large portion of his piece. His nut began to bubble. "Aww, fuck! Here it cums. Ssshit!" He growled as he bucked and unloaded big globs of cum into her mouth.

He gripped the side of her head tightly. She gulped and swallowed his entire load. "Oooh, shit. Oooh, shit . . . Damn!" Corey panted, as Sandra tenderly licked around the crown of his cock, making sure to get all the excess goo.

Once satisfied, she popped him out of her mouth, checked herself in the visor, then stepped out of the car. Corey watched as she walked down the street, ass twitching. He shook his head. He definitely needed to get another dose of that. *Smoker or not!* Corey slid his piece back in and headed to the store.

Once he got there, he grabbed what he needed, jumped back in the Lac, and decided to take the backstreets. As soon as he made a right onto the street the trap was on, his heart dropped. Cops. Everywhere.

Not just cops, but unmarked vehicles. *Detectives.* Sure enough, he noticed plain-clothes detectives walking to and from the trap. Corey backed up and found somewhere discrete to park. He got out and walked, opting to stay hidden behind the fence line of trees. From his vantage point, he could see the front of the trap. But, they couldn't see him.

He watched in horror as detectives brought out an angry and irate Happy. Handcuffed and belligerent. What struck Corey as odd was that Keeno was being let go. He took off walking down the street. *It couldn't have been a drug bust,* Corey concluded.

Corey stayed hidden as they shoved Happy in an unmarked car and whisked him away. Once the coast was clear, he walked back to the car, hopped in and hightailed it back to the crib.

Tee Tee was at work, and wouldn't get off until around 5 p.m. Corey knew Happy would call, as soon as he made it to the County. All he could do was wait.

Five-thirty came and Tee Tee was walking in from work. "Happy! Happy! Come help me with these groceries," she yelled. Tee Tee saw the Lac, and figured Happy was the one driving.

Corey was sitting on the couch, trying to figure out how he should tell her. "Hey, Corey. Can you help me with these bags?" she asked him. "I know Happy's lazy ass is probably back there asleep."

"Actually. Happy's locked up, Tee." She dropped the bags she was carrying. Her jaw dropped.

"What! For what?"

"I don't know. We were at the trap earlier. I went to the store. When I came back, there were laws everywhere," Corey reported.

"Oh my God. Please don't tell me this." She began to pace frantically. Finally, she sat down on the couch.

Corey didn't know what to say to console her. "Umm, look. I'm 'bout to go grab the bags out of the car. I'm pretty sure he's gonna call soon. When he does, tell him to let me know what he wants me to do," Corey told her before walking out to grab the groceries.

Once all the groceries were put up, they waited, Happy didn't call until close to 9 o'clock. He told Tee Tee they had him on a bogus ass murder charge. Someone got killed at the middle school, and they're trying to say he did it. He assured her everything was a mistake, and not to worry, it would get sorted out.

After two twenty-minute phone calls with her, Happy asked to speak with Corey. "Hello?"

"Wassup, Kinfolk?"

"Same ole shit. Tee Tee told me what they're trynna put on you."

"Yeah? Shit's crazy, my nigga. Remember that play station controller you borrowed to play Call of Duty?" Happy was speaking code. Referencing the gun Corey used to kill Pig.

"Yeah, I do. The one I gave back to you. Right?"

"Yeah, Yeah. That one. Shit's crazy, bruh." *They have the murder weapon.* "Man, they got a nigga walking round in sandals and shit."

"Man, gone on. For real? What happened to your J's?" Corey asked, already knowing the answer.

"That's what I'm saying. You know, them hoes wasn't the regular Cool Gray's. A nigga paid three hundred and fifty dollars for them bitches." *They got the shoes he wore on the night of the murder,* Corey realized.

"So, what you need me to do?" Corey was almost too afraid to ask.

"Shit. Right now, I need you to hook up with Keeno. We got a call from Ms. Gladys." Ms. Gladys was the old lady that stayed down the street from the trap. She'd seen the laws forming up at the barber shop, and called Happy. By the time the laws pulled up, all the drugs had been relocated. *But Happy had forgotten the gun, under the couch cushion.*

"Y'all gotta keep the house in order. Imma put you on my boy Pablo. He's gon' make sure you're good. Just make sure *I'm* good, Kinfolk." Happy wanted Corey to take over the trap. He was plugging him in with the connect. In return, Corey would have to break Happy off.

"That's *ovastood*. I got you, my nigga. On me," Corey pledged.

"Let me holla at Tee Tee's ass one more time.

"A'ight, bro. Love, nigga."

"Love," Happy replied, before Corey gave Tee the phone. She grabbed it, then walked into the bedroom. She locked eyes with Corey before closing her bedroom door.

Five days later, Corey was in the trap, pumping *hard*, *soft*, and K-2. After linking up with Pablo, Corey got fronted a half a brick. That was three days ago. He was almost out. Down to his last couple onions. He planned on frying one, then bagging the other.

Just as he was about to pick up the phone and dial Pablo, Tee Tee called. "Hello?"

"Hey, Corey. I know you're busy, but I was 'bout to cook something. I didn't know what, so what you feel like eating?"

"Uhh. How 'bout some smothered chops, and some dirty rice."

"I can do that," she told him. "What time you plan on coming home?"

Corey looked at his watch. One he *borrowed* from Happy. "Give me like an hour and a half. I gotta go holla at P, real quick."

"See you then," she said, before hanging up. Corey had to admit, it felt good going home to a home cooked meal, after a hard day of grinding. Even though the home wasn't his, or the woman doing the cooking, for that matter. Still, it felt good.

Corey whipped and bagged the last two zips, then left them to Keeno to grind. He needed to link up with Pablo. This time, he was going to purchase a half, and also get fronted a half.

When he finally made it back to the house, the sweet aroma of a home cooked meal assaulted his senses. He found Tee Tee in the kitchen, putting the finishing touches on the masterpiece.

She had on a pair of Men's Perry Ellis boxers. They were so tight on her, they looked like Biker shorts. She also had on a Houston Astros jersey. Corey could tell from the shape of her nipples protruding through the mesh material, Tee didn't have on a bra. She turned when she heard him enter. "Oh, hey, Corey. Dinner's almost ready," she said cheerfully.

He couldn't help but bite his lip at the sight of her. Her booty was looking soft, and . . . oh, so heavy. "Bet. Let me shower first," he said, heading to the only bathroom in the house. The one attached to Happy and Tee's bedroom.

Once Corey was done, he walked back into the dining room. The table was already set for two. Tee was standing by the table, talking on the phone. She held up a finger to her lips, signaling Corey to be quiet. "No. Corey's not here yet. He should be at the trap. A'ight. I'll let him know." Obviously, she was talking to Happy. Corey's face slightly contorted at the lie she just told."

Corey didn't understand why she felt she needed to lie about something so trivial. Tee must have read his mind. "Look. Only reason I said that was because I'd already told him I was cooking. He asked if I was cooking for you too. I told him no, you weren't even here. If I would have said I *was* cooking for you, he would have accused me of trynna suck your dick or something. Happy's ass could be so extra sometimes," Tee Tee argued. "He's probably 'bout to call your phone next."

Sure enough, Corey's phone rang. He really didn't want to lie to his kinfolk about something so small, but he couldn't expose Tee Tee like that. "Hello? Yeah, what's good . . . I just left Pablo's. I'm 'bout to put the shit up and probably head to your crib. Huh? More than likely, I'll grab some Church's on the way home. Why? . . . Oh, I don't know if she's cooking or not. She be cooking for herself. Yeah. I got you. Imma shoot her five bands to put towards your lawyer. That's a bet. Love." Corey hung the phone up, feeling like a fraud. That was a useless lie.

He and Tee Tee started eating. Then, she poured them both a glass of Crown and Coke, and began to ask about him. How he grew up in the city of Houston, and went on to tell him about life in the country. How she yearned for more excitement in her life. She said she'd visited Houston plenty of times. Usually, it was to shop.

"A while back, you was saying how you was trynna get Happy to put you down with a female. Did you ever get your dick wet?" The question threw Corey off a bit. He damn near choked on his pork chop.

He didn't expect her to ask. And if she did, he didn't expect her to ask *like* that. Corey neglected to count the smoker that topped him off, and sheepishly told her: "No, I haven't."

Tee stared at him for what seemed like eternity. Suddenly, she stood up, then sat by him on the love seat. Without so much as a word, she reached inside of his shorts, gripped his dick in her warm, small hands, and pulled him out.

Everything inside him was screaming out: *What you're both doing is foul as fuck. For crying out loud—this is your cousin's girlfriend.* But, a part of him always knew it would happen. Tee Tee jacked his dick while she talked to him. "Look. Happy's in jail. I'm not with that fucking-random-ass-niggas shit. You're already here. I say we take care of each other until Happy comes home. *Then*, we go our separate ways." Tee Tee purred, as she stroked him to full attention.

Corey could barely concentrate, much less form a reply. He would have agreed to anything, to feel her warm mouth, or wet pussy, covering his cock. "Sssshit, Tee. I'm for that. But, I'm not trynna fuck up what y'all got going. You know, Happy's my guy," he told her.

"Oh, trust. Happy and I are forever. I just need my kitty scratched while he's gone. Better you than some off brand nigga. Right?" Before Corey could nod, she dived onto his dick. His cock fit snug into her mouth. Corey's shoulders slumped as he gave into her oral onslaught.

Tee Tee slurped, sucked, licked and spat on the dick. She dipped under his nut sack, placing each one of his balls into her mouth. "Ooh, shit," Corey moaned, as a chill crawled up his spine. Her tongue danced back and forth, traveling further down south until it teased at his back door.

She hopped off the couch and knelt in front of him. Completely submissive, she pushed one of his legs back. His left foot planted flat on the couch cushion. His right, still rooted on the ground. His balls dangled, low and free.

Tee Tee's phone rang. It was the ring tone she assigned for the jail. She thought to ignore it, but she knew he wouldn't stop calling. Then, he would be all in her ass about it. With Corey's dick in her left hand, the phone in her right, she answered. "Hello? She waited and pressed "0" to accept the call. "Heyy, baby," she cooed, as she lightly pecked on Corey's nut sack

Corey felt some type of way about the blatant disrespect Tee Tee was showing. Still, his desires outweighed his conscience. The act reminded him of Ty, and how she would do her baby daddy when he used to call from jail. Women like that are what prevented Corey from settling down. "Uhm . . . He's in the living room . . . I think he's sleeping . . . You want me to go give him the phone?" she finessed.

Corey assumed he said no, because Tee went right back to sucking and kissing on his balls. It seemed like that phone call was the longest twenty minutes ever.

Once the call had ended, Tee Tee hung the phone up and began to deep-throat Corey's sizeable cock. He palmed the back of her head, and aggressively fucked her face. The rest of the night was spent with them sexing each other's brains out. She let him have his way with her. Corey even got to hit her in that nice, round, fluffy ass of hers.

After the first round in the living room, Corey smashed her on the bed she and Happy shared. He came all in her mouth. Over her face. On her ass and in her pussy. When it was said and done, daylight was peeking through the blinds. Both of them were sleeping in each other's arms, sweaty, sticky, without a care in the world.

It'd been a week and a half since Chief had kidnapped Jeremiah. The young boy was hanging by a thread. Trapped in the closet. *Literally.* Pat was combing the streets looking for him. His school had been wondering what had happened; so were the authorities. No one had seen or heard from him.

Mya was distraught. For five days straight, she hadn't been to school. This was her first day back.

As she was walking out of the building, she expected Marcus to be waiting for her. Instead, Chief pulled up. In a late model, navy blue, Jaguar. *His mother's.*

Of course, Mya didn't need to know all that. Marcus had been working overtime to try and catch Pat slipping. But, Pat moved like the president, so it was taking longer than expected. Because of that, Chief volunteered to scoop Mya up. He had very special plans for her.

When Mya saw the Jag, she began to blush. Chief made a big show of getting out and opening up the door for her. Her classmates looked at her as if she was some type of celebrity. "Where's Marcus?" she asked, as she slid onto the Italian leather.

"He had some really important bidness to attend to. What? You don't want me to take you home?" Chief feigned annoyance.

"Oh, naw. It's nothing like that. I was just asking." Truth be told, she was very attracted to Chief. If she wasn't already involved with Jeremiah, Chief could have definitely got it. Thinking about Jeremiah made her heart ache.

"Well, I'm glad to hear that. If you don't mind, we need to make a few stops before I take you home," Chief informed her, while leaving the school parking lot.

"Boy, you good. My momma ain't doing no trippin'. She knows you, so you a'ight." Even though he was only a couple years older, Mya felt Chief was a full-grown man. She didn't want him to view her as some little girl who couldn't go where she wanted, when she wanted.

"Bet. First stop, you hungry?" Mya's stomach growled at the mention of food.

"Not really, but we can stop to grab something to eat," she lied. Chief stopped at a BBQ spot on Wallisville, called Ray's. They ordered their food, then sat at the picnic tables the restaurant kept outside.

As Mya got up to take a call from one of her classmates, Chief pulled out a vial with some off colored powder in it. He popped it open, then poured the contents in her soft drink.

A few minutes later, Mya returned to finish her meal. Once the meal was devoured, the two of them hopped back into the car. This time, Chief could tell the difference in her demeanor. She kept licking her lips. Her legs kept opening and closing like butterfly wings. She constantly kept rubbing her palms on her thighs. "You a'ight over there?" Chief slyly asked.

Mya felt the vibrations of his voice all in her coochie. She tried to adjust the A/C. She'd never felt the way she was feeling, ever before. She began to nod off. At the same time, her pussy wouldn't stop cumming. When she came to, her and Chief were in front of an old raggedy looking house.

He was saying something about buying it and fixing it up. It sounded as if he'd asked her if she wanted to see inside. She didn't remember saying yes, but suddenly they were walking through the front door.

The house was filthy. The smell of mold was so heavy that Mya began to choke until she got used to it. Chief told her the house had been severely damaged in the last hurricane. The efforts to restore it had been abandoned.

Chief led Mya to a room in the back. There was a pallet on the floor, with a pillow resting on top of it. He suddenly kissed Mya on her neck. Her brain was telling her to rebuff his advances, but her body had already given in. A slight moan escaped her lips.

He nibbled on her earlobe, and she was lost. Seconds later, Mya was butt naked, with her legs cocked back, behind her head. Chief gripped the back of her thighs tightly, as he dug in her coochie. Long, powerful strokes. Mya barely knew where she was at, but she knew she was cumming. "Oh shit. Oh shit, I'm finna cummmm!"

"Cum on this dick, Mya. Cum all over this big ass dick," Chief urged. Her body shook, as her orgasm tore her apart. Chief moved her legs, and put them over his shoulders. Her titties popped out of her tee, as he showed her no mercy.

"Oh my gawd, Chief! You finna make me cum again. Oh no, not again. Fuck. This dick is so good. I'm cumming, I'm cumming, I'm cummmminng." Mya howled as she came for the umpteenth time. She'd never felt anything like this. This was the best dick she'd ever had in her life. And she told Chief that same thing, right before he pulled out and came all over her face and tongue.

Chief wasn't done. He dick'd her down until she was unconscious. When she shook back, she was in her driveway. If it wasn't for the fact her body was aching, and the cum on her breath, she would've thought it was all a dream.

She glanced at the time. *9:30 p.m.* She'd left school at 2:30. *Damn. Time flew by.*

Meanwhile, back at the abandoned house, Jeremiah cried. Having to be forced to watch the love of his life fuck another dude. To witness her do things and allow things to be done to her body that even he hadn't tried. He'd hope that Mya would find a way to convince her mom to let him go. Now it seemed Mya could care less. Even though Ty told him she didn't know, he knew now, that was a lie. How could she not? If he survived, he would make them all pay. Somehow, he didn't believe he would.

Chapter 13

After days of stalking, Marcus still hadn't found his window of opportunity. Due to the Intel Chief *squeezed* out of Jeremiah, Marcus knew where Pat's wife, Jamiyah's momma, stayed. He figured, since he couldn't get to Pat, he'd settle for the next best thing.

He learned every other weekend, Jaliyah would go visit her mother. She would always take her three-year-old daughter, Jamiyah with her. This particular weekend was no different.

Marcus paid a smoker to use his Toyota Corolla. He and Chief were parked down the street from Pat's mother in-law. Waiting.

"What we gon' do? Hold them for ransom? If so, how much," Chief asked, as he played idly with his P89 Ruger.

"Yeah, but I don't know how much yet. I'd asked Ty, but I don't even think she knows," Marcus responded honestly. Marcus felt as if Ty could care less about the money. She just wanted Pat to suffer. There had been a drastic change, since CJ's body had been discovered. First, it was utter depression. Then, when she found out it was Pat behind it, depression turned into determination. So, it was up to Marcus to think about the future.

All Ty cared about was sating her revenge. Even her touch had become cold and detached. Each time they had sex, it seemed as if Ty was trying to hurt herself with the dick. She would choke until she threw up. She would beg him to fuck her until she bled. Sex for Marcus was beginning to become unenjoyable.

Marcus and Chief sat and waited. Finally, Jaliyah emerged from the house, with her daughter in tow. "Damn. No cap. Dude's wife bad!" Chief commented. She had a pink and yellow sundress on. Even though the dress was modest, they could both see she was packing a hell of a body underneath. Jaliyah had her hair pinned up. Exposing her natural beauty. No one could deny, Pat's wife was definitely something to look at.

"So, look," Marcus began. "We'll wait until she gets on Florence Street. Right before she tries to get on the freeway. You jump out and snatch her ass up. I'll get the lil girl," Marcus told him.

The pair sat back and watched, as Jaliyah strapped and buckled little Jamiyah in. Marcus cranked the car up, and put it in drive. He made the turn, and waited for her to ease out of her mother's driveway. They already knew the route she would take. They sped up, then laid in wait for her.

Before she knew it, her bumper was a mere four feet away from their fender. Smoke arose from the asphalt, as her car came inches away from colliding with theirs. Her eyes were wide in shock. Her hands trembled.

Jaliyah immediately turned around in her seat, checking on her baby girl. Her heart thundered in her chest. Her rib cage rattled. Now that she knew her daughter was safe, she had a serious bone to pick with the occupants of the next car.

She shot out of the car, eager to give whoever was in the other car a piece of her mind. What she wasn't expecting was a man with a gun, yelling for her to open the door. Jaliyah screamed.

Glass shattered. "Bitch, shut up. Before I kill you and that brat," he growled. He reached in and unlocked the door for himself. After unbuckling her safety belt, he yanked Jaliyah out of the car, and marched her towards the Corolla.

"My daughter. Please. I have a daughter," she begged.

"Don't worry. She's coming too," he assured her. Marcus had already hopped out of the car, and was headed to go snatch up little Jamiyah. The little girl wailed for her mother. Not fully understanding what was transpiring, but sensing her mother's distress.

Chief snatched the back door of the Corolla open, then shoved Jaliyah into the backseat. Shutting the door closed, Marcus placed her daughter into the front seat. He hopped in the driver seat, and mashed on the gas. All that took less than a minute. No one noticed a thing.

Meanwhile, Pat was at one of his duck offs on the North West. He'd bought a townhome in Spring Branch. No one knew about it, except for his closest Lieutenants, J-P and Byrd. He was currently having a closed door meeting with the both of them.

It'd been close to a week since his nephew had come up missing. His gut was telling him, Ty and that young nigga had something to do with it. He didn't think that they knew he was behind her son getting kidnapped. But, what if they do? What if Meme had spilled the beans? He was still out looking for her.

She hadn't been back to her apartment since. And just a while back, that lame ass nigga she was fucking with was found dead with his dome pushed in. He should have *parked* Meme when he had the chance.

Now, he was losing sleep behind it. But, she would have to take a back seat, because now, his main objective was finding his nephew. "What they talkin' 'bout out there?" Pat asked J-P. J-P was a bright-skinned young nigga from Fort Worth, who came to Houston a few years ago. At the time, Pat was looking for a new shooter. J-P showed his worth. Since then, his loyalty and dedication ensured him a top spot. Now, Pat entrusted him with probably the most important mission ever. *Finding his nephew.*

"Nothing, my nigga. I pushed up on a few niggas on his football team. I had one of the lil homies try and holla at his girl. He told me she'd been so fucked up about it, she hadn't been to school in days. Right now, ain't nobody seen nothing," J-P, explained.

Pat definitely wasn't feeling that. He was used to being in control of all the variables. Since the situation with Ty's son, he'd been laying low, especially since Meme was still on the loose. Now, he was thinking maybe he should poke his head out of the foxhole. *Maybe the reason I'm not getting the right answers is because the right nigga isn't asking the questions.*

Pat studied his two lieutenants for a second, before he voiced his intentions. "Tell the team, we're going out tomorrow night. We'll hit *Club Heat* up, twenty deep," he told them. "In the meantime, we *do not* stop looking for my nephew. I know if I'm out and about, the top niggas in the city gon' come out. If not for nothing else, but to try and outshine a nigga. We'll see what they done heard." J-P and Byrd nodded, before grabbing their things and departing.

Once he was alone, Pat picked up his phone and dialed his wife, Jaliyah. It went to voicemail, so he texted. He let her know he was coming *back* to the city. Surely, she would hear about his outing at the club on social media.

To explain his absence, he'd told her he had to go out of town. Supposedly, that's where he'd been this whole time. He hated to lie to her, but he felt it was for the best. The less she knew, the better. Pat waited for ten minutes. Still, no reply.

He looked at the time and realized she may still be at her mother's house. *She'll hit back when she sees my text.*

Pat leaned back on the couch and closed his eyes. The mental exhaustion took over. Soon, he was in a deep sleep.

Twenty-four hours later, Pat still hadn't talked to his wife. The unknown made him paranoid as hell. He'd told his team to spread the word through social media. *Pat is back!* Now, he wasn't so sure that was a good idea.

He finally called his mother in-law. She said she hadn't heard from Jaliyah since the day before, "When she left with my grandbaby." Pat went by the house. Her car was missing. Now her phone was going straight to voicemail. As if the battery had died.

Pat had a very eerie feeling. He *wasn't* about to call the cops and report her missing. *Fuck twelve!* He didn't need their help for shit. He contemplated canceling the outing, but said *fuck that!* He couldn't tuck his tail. Pat was a Boss, and Bosses don't buckle. They buck under pressure. He just prayed his wife and his daughter were safe, wherever they were.

Club Heat was packed, as usual. Pat and his crew made sure they valeted the whips. As soon as they walked in, the DJ announced their arrival. Uno, the manager, escorted them to VIP and made sure they had two bottles of *Ace of Spades* brought to them. And of course, Pat told him to bring 18 more.

He wanted each member of his crew to have their own bottle. This was his *welcome back* party. He wasn't about to half step it. Something caught his eye. A woman who looked strongly familiar. They locked eyes for the briefest of moments. He could have sworn he'd just seen Meme. He tried frantically to see if it was in fact her. But, by the time the crowd dissipated, the woman was gone.

He contemplated leaving VIP, and trying to see if he could hunt the woman down. Then, he thought better of it. *I'll catch up with her,* he assured himself.

While he and his crew were partying, many of the city's top niggas pulled up to pay their respects. Pat was a rising star in the city, and many wanted to hitch a ride with him to the top. He used the time to inquire about his nephew. He hadn't mentioned his wife yet. He prayed she was just upset, and avoiding his calls. He tried to push it out of his mind and enjoy the night. Everything will work out.

"Girl . . . What's wrong with you?" Laura shrieked, as Meme kept pulling on her arm. They'd been enjoying themselves, when out of nowhere, Meme made a mad dash for the exit. Now, they were shuffling through the parking lot, trying to remember where they parked.

"Bitch. That was my X. I can't be in there with him right now. The nigga's obsessed as shit," Meme claimed. "The last time I saw him, he tried to kill me. *Literally.*" The lies kept rolling off her tongue.

She didn't know what type of timing Pat was on, but she sure didn't want to stick around and find out. "Okay. Okay. But stop pulling on my arm. You 'bout to dislocate my shit," Laura said, only half joking. They finally came to a stop.

"Oh, my bad. It's just . . . That nigga's dangerous. With a capital D. If he had seen me, I wouldn't have made it out of there." Meme was laying it on thick.

Laura seemed skeptical. "Girl. I don't think that nigga is that crazy to try and do something to you *inside* the club," she pointed out.

"*He* probably won't, but he has an army of flunkies willing to do his bidding."

"Which one was he?"

"The nigga in VIP with the creme colored Versace shirt."

Laura looked mildly surprised. "You talking about the one the DJ introduced?" Meme looked confused. "Oh, yeah. You were in the restroom when he and his boys walked in." The nervousness on Meme's face was apparent. "A'ight, girl. We ain't gotta be in there, but we look too damn good to go home. So, I say we go downtown and check out what's popping there." Meme agreed, and the women hopped in their matching Jag's and took their show on the road.

"Man, I'm telling you, my nigga. I heard it loud and clear. That nigga's at *Club Heat,*" Chief reassured Marcus, as they sped down I-10.

Earlier, Chief happened to be on the phone with his mom, trying to see what time she would be back so he could use her car, when he overheard the DJ in the background, shouting out Pat and his crew. After asking her what club she was at, Chief had a location.

He couldn't wait to call Marcus. Now, they were loaded up and headed West. This was the chance they'd been waiting on. A chance to finally spank Pat.

Since they were rushing, the two were only able to grab a couple handguns and the micro Draco. They honestly didn't have a plan, other than waiting on him to leave the club. Obviously. They didn't know how deep he was moving. What they did know, though, he wasn't alone. "Look, Bro, we gon' park across the street. We ain't gon' hit him at the club. It's where he will be at his strongest. Plus, we don't want the club's cameras catching shit. We're gonna try and slide on him on the freeway," Marcus told Chief.

Marcus drove up there, but once they arrived, they switched seats. They'd agreed that Marcus would get the honors of twisting Pat's wig back. It was only right. He owed him a bullet in the head. Not to mention, Marcus was the one who set off the chain of events.

While they waited, both hopped on the social media pages. Sure enough, people were posting *live* from *Club Heat*. Luckily, some random female recorded Pat in VIP, flexing hard. Now, thanks to her, they knew exactly what he had on.

Twenty minutes before the club closed, Pat came out staggering. All their cars were valeted, so it was easy for Pat to be spotted. Marcus steadied his breathing. Of course, this wasn't the first time he'd peeled a nigga's shit back. He had enough bodies under his belt to label him a professional killer. But this, by far, was the most significant.

He snatched the Draco and sat it on his lap. His Glock .21 was loaded and on the floor between his feet. Marcus traveled deep within himself. He replaced the decent, caring young man, with the cold-blooded killer. No words, just action.

Chief waited until Pat's triple black, Bentley Continental maneuvered out the parking lot. They didn't want to play him too close. They knew they only had one shot. Marcus told himself, even if he had to die to make sure Pat paid, *so be it.*

Chief hopped onto Richmond. Their convoy headed to the 610 loop. He was three cars behind the Bentley and Pat was riding shotgun. Chief tried to maneuver to give Marcus the best shot, but it was a very busy street. "Catch the light," Marcus urged. Chief swerved around a car, barely catching the light.

Now, it was only Pat's Bentley and two more cars from their crew. "Fuck it. I'm 'bout to spank him at the next light," Marcus declared coldly, as if he was a surgeon about to perform a routine surgery.

Marcus pulled the lever, and leaned the passenger seat all the way back. He rolled his window all the way down. The light before the overpass showed red.

Chief pulled up next to the Bentley. He paid close attention to the intersecting lights. Once he saw the opposing traffic light go yellow, and the cars slow down, he knew their light was soon to turn green. Two seconds later, it did. "Eat!"

Marcus raised up from his reclining position. The Draco began to sing; .762's spun through the barrel. *'Pap. Pap. Pap. Pap.'* The driver side window on the Bentley shattered.

"Oh, shit. Fuck!" Marcus heard the panicked cries from someone in Pat's vehicle. *'Bocka! Bocka! Bocka!'* The rear windshield on the Corolla splintered, then broke into a hundred fragments.

One of the cars behind saw what was going on and decided to come to Pat's aid. *'Bocka. Bocka.'* A shot whizzed by Marcus's face. He felt the searing heat from the slug, the gun powder and hot metal leaving a distinct aroma.

Marcus wanted to *walk* Pat down. He needed to make sure he was dead. But, he knew the element of surprise was gone.

He would probably be dead before he could reach Pat's car. Plus, now they were causing too much attention. He would have to just hope he put in enough work to get the job down.

He'd let off a whole 30 clip. At least half went into the car's frame. *That should be more than enough,* he surmised. The light turned green. Chief smashed on the gas pedal. *'Bocka. Bocka. Bocka.'* Marcus ducked down, and looked back.

Pat's crew was hot on their trail. "Fuck! Say, take them to the East," Marcus yelled, as he climbed into the backseat. He peered over the rear head rest with the Draco and let it rip. *'Pap. Pap. Pap. Pap. Pap.'* . . . *'Bocka. Bocka. Bocka.'*

Shots were being traded, right on the middle of the freeway. *'Clink. Clink.'* Bullets pierced through the trunk of the dope fiend rental. Chief swung from lane to lane, trying to outrun the two SUVs trailing.

The highway was empty. They were the only three vehicles, for at least a hundred yards. Chief decided to exit. Try his luck on some residential streets.

He exited Mercury and made a right through Jacinto City. *'Bocka. Bocka. Bocka.'* A shot went through the shattered back windshield, cracking the front. Marcus continued to fire off the Draco until he ran empty. Then, he grabbed his Glock and let that bark. "Go through Clinton Park," he screamed.

Chief turned down Market, then made a quick left over the railroad tracks. The SUVs pursued. Shots continued to ring out. Marcus ducked down and called his nigga Boo on the phone. "Hello? Say, Boo, I got these niggas following me . . . Bet!"

Marcus grabbed his Glock and fired two shots. Just to keep them honest. "Say, Chief, go down North Carolina, they gon' be out there, waiting." *'POP!'* One of the tires blew out, and Chief almost lost control.

Miraculously, he made the turn onto North Carolina. They could see Boo and the others, posted on each side of the street. Waiting. Each of them looked as if they had sticks, dangling at their sides.

The drivers of the SUVs must have seen the same thing, because they smashed on their brakes, reversed and got the hell out of Dodge.

Chief pulled up to the house, stopped and killed the engine. He and Marcus hopped out, hugging and laughing maniacally. They barely escaped. They were delirious with joy. Boo walked up, looking at both of them inquisitively. "Man, what the fuck y'all niggas got going on?" Marcus took the time to lace him up on what he felt Boo needed to know. As he did, he was praying Pat was dead.

Marcus and Chief stood back and took a good look at the Corolla. Bullet holes decorated the car's frame. The tail lights were busted. The back windshield shattered. The front windshield cracked. Even the rear left tire was shredded. It was a miracle they survived. If they had stayed on the freeway, they would have been easy targets.

Boo invited them in. After a couple of blunts, Ty arrived to come scoop them up. They dropped Chief off at his mom's crib, then headed home for the night.

Chief had gotten dropped off and noticed two Jaguars in the driveway. One of them was his mom's. *Whose was the other?* he wondered. As he walked in, he saw his mom reclining in her chair, while a light-skinned woman sat with her legs crossed on the love seat. They were both sipping drinks, listening to Keisha Cole. "Oh, heyy, baby," Laura called out.

"Hey, momma," Chief answered, but kept his eyes on her guest. Laura saw what had her son captivated, so she took the time to introduce the two.

"Calvin, this my girl Meme . . . Meme, this is my son . . . Calvin." Chief looked at his momma, annoyed. He always hated when she introduced him by his government name.

"Well, well, nice to meet you, Mr. Calvin," Meme purred. Chief was taken back on how forward she was with her flirtation in front of his mom. He took notice of the glasses of wine they were sipping on. He could tell, they were both lit.

Something kept nagging at Chief's mental. Right at the surface, but he couldn't figure it out. Then, it hit him. *Meme!* That was the same name Marcus said stole the money he and Ty had been saving up. He needed to be sure. But how?

After the introductions, he complained about being hungry, then stumbled into the kitchen. Now that the adrenaline wore off, his body ached. He felt sluggish. Chief began to fix himself a sandwich. When Meme took her attention off of him, Chief pulled his phone out and recorded a three second video. He sent it to Marcus, with the subject: *Is this Meme?*

No longer than fifteen seconds later, he got a thumbs up emoji, with the text: *Where did you see her at?*

Chief responded: *At my house right now!*

Marcus: *OTW*

Chief: *Naw. I got it. Trust.*

Marcus: *Bet.*

Chief ended the conversation, grabbed his sandwich and went back into the living room with the women. After twenty minutes, Laura took notice of the chemistry between the two. She excused herself, so they could at least talk. "So . . . Mr. Calvin, your mom tells me you just got out of jail."

"Yeah, I did. And please call me Chief, all my friends do." Meme smiled at that. "How do you know my mom?"

"We met at *Club Heat*." Chief sat up straight.

"Y'all met tonight, at *Club Heat*?"

"Oh, naw, naw. We met some weeks ago. We've been kicking it ever since." As an afterthought, she added. "We *were* up there tonight though, but we had left early."

"Oh, okay." Chief was relieved. They spent about an hour talking, before Meme decided to take it home. She was feeling the young nigga, but wasn't about to buss it open on the first night. Even though she and Laura had been freaking niggas together, she had a lot of respect and admiration for the slightly older woman.

Laura's money was legit. And, she was making it the right way. Meme secretly idolized Laura, and she didn't want to move too fast with her son. They exchanged numbers with the promise to meet up again soon.

As she stood up, Chief got a good look at her body. Breathtaking. She was definitely stacked. Thick in all the right places. Plus, she was cute as hell. Not to mention, she had that banana red complexion. Chief had a thing for bright women.

After she left, Chief called Marcus and relayed the encounter he had with Meme. Together, they came up with a plan. As Chief laid in bed, thinking about Meme and what they had in store for her, he thought to himself, *Damn. I need to make sure I tap that at least once before she dies.*

Chapter 14

It'd been a month since Happy went to jail for murdering Pig. He still had a "No Bond". But, Corey had been breaking him off every week, while he worked the trap.

He'd also been breaking Happy's girlfriend Tee Tee off with that dick, every chance he got. Corey had gotten so bold as to ride around in Happy's "El Dog", while Tee Tee domed him up. Many times, Happy had called Corey's phone, thinking he was out and about. The whole time, he was at the house, with his dick in Tee Tee's mouth.

At first, Corey had felt bad about it. Especially since Happy was technically locked up for a murder Corey committed. But, what Tee Tee said made sense. She was going to be out there fucking anyway. It might as well be him to scratch that itch.

Pablo had just blessed him with two birds. One he paid for and the other on consignment. He needed to head to the stash house first. He planned on putting one up, then bussing the other one down. Half hard, and half soft. The way the trap was booming, a brick would only last three to four days.

Corey pulled up to the corner store to grab some blunt wraps and some snacks. When he came out, he noticed a late model, navy blue, Chevy Cobalt parked across the street.

He tried to peer through the front windshield to see who was driving. But, it appeared as if the front windshield was slightly tinted. A chill went up his spine. He thought about the bricks he had, plus the pistol.

His heart began to gallop in his chest. He steadied his breathing. He didn't want to appear nervous. *Maybe I'm tripping,* he thought. Corey unlocked the Lac, hopped it and strapped on his seat belt. The bricks were secured in a false panel, in the trunk. The Glock, on the other hand, was right there in the passenger seat.

He quickly scooped it up, and placed it in his lap. If he had to make a run, he wanted to make sure he had it with him. He cranked the car up, said a quick prayer, then turned out of the parking lot.

Sure enough. As soon as he passed the Chevy Cobalt up, they turned around and got behind him. Now he *knew* he wasn't tripping. He didn't want to give them any undue reason to mess with him, so he hit his right blinker before making his turn. One more block, before he got into the neighborhood.

If they waited to pull him over then, he told himself he would take them on a foot chase. He checked the rearview to see if any other cars had joined the pursuit. So far, it was just the Chevy. *Good!*

He went to make the last turn, then out of nowhere, two Tahoes came to a screeching halt in front of him. Corey had to smash on the breaks to avoid a collision. As soon as the Lac came to a stop, the doors to the Tahoes swung open. U.S. Marshals emerged, assault rifles up and at the ready.

They were screaming. "Put your hands on the wheel! On the wheel now!" They stalked towards him. Corey was frozen stuck. With the pistol in his lap, he had the option of grabbing it and letting loose, but his common sense kicked in.

As far as he knew, this could be drug related. If so, it wasn't worth holding court behind. He did the sensible thing. He put his hands on the steering wheel. The Marshals yanked the driver door open, and snatched him out of the car.

Without question, they slapped the cuffs on him. As they were shoving him into the backseat of one of the Tahoes,

Corey glanced around. *Barbie!* The last thing he saw, before they shut the door. She was standing on the sidewalk, with a smirk on her face.

The U.S. Marshals didn't read him his rights. They waited until he'd gotten downtown. A homicide detective met him in booking.

"Corey Mosley. You're under arrest for the murders of Kourtney Jamison and Elizabeth Price. You have the right . . ." Corey's heart dropped. He was praying all this was about dope. Or even about Pig's murder. At least he would've known, he had action there. But Kourtney? His baby momma? If he got picked up, that means they have something. Not knowing *what,* frightened him.

Three weeks after he was booked in, Corey went to his initial hearing. His court-appointed attorney really didn't tell him much. Supposedly, they had an eye witness who saw him shoot his baby momma and her best friend. No doubt, it was one of those geeked up smokers, who lived in Beaumont Place.

He told his court-appointed to reset him for as far away as possible. He needed time to put some money together, so he could hire a real lawyer. He didn't have much. He'd just spent $26k on that key, plus he owed the connect 28k, for the one he got fronted. Corey kept his bread under the couch, at Happy's crib. He just hoped he could trust Tee Tee.

On his way back from court, they placed him in a holding cell. He walked in, and couldn't believe his eyes. "Maannn. What the fuck?" Happy cried out, when he saw Corey. They gave each other a hug. Happy made the dude sitting next to him scoop over, so Corey could sit.

Corey felt nervous around Happy. He'd been fucking his cousin's woman. Now that he was face to face with him, Corey couldn't look him in the eye. "Damn, my nigga. I called Tee Tee, and she told me they had snatched you up for

146

something. She just didn't know for what." Happy still couldn't believe it.

"Yeah. They got me for that shit I was telling you about," Corey informed him. "What they talkin' 'bout with your shit?"

"Right now, they ain't talking 'bout shit. It's still early. My lawyer got affidavits from some of the people from the party. Especially Deedra. They got the bitch ass pistol, and blood splatters on my shoes I ain't even know was there. I should have gotten rid of the gun, though."

"But wait. How the fuck did they know to pull up on you?" Happy asked.

"That, I don't know. When they ran down on us at the spot, I thought it was 'bout some dope. Then, they hit a nigga with murder warrant. Like I said, it's still early. I told my lawyer, I didn't do it. So, he asked me who did."

Corey lifted his head up. This was the first time he'd look Happy square in his eyes since he came into the holding tank. "What you tell them?"

"Nigga, what you mean? I ain't tell them shit. That's my lawyer, but I don't trust that nigga." Corey couldn't hide his relief. He had his own shit to shovel. Happy saw the relief on Corey's face and couldn't help but to feel some type of way. Any hope of Corey being a real nigga and taking his lick looked dim.

Happy was a thorough nigga. He wasn't about to fold, but damn . . . This was a hard pill to swallow. "Tee Tee's ass is supposed to come up here and see a nigga today," Happy said. Corey flinched at the mention of Tee Tee, but he didn't notice it. "What was she out there doing?" He couldn't resist asking.

"Shit. She was chillin', dawg. Talkin' 'bout how she missed you. She barely left the house." Just as Corey said it, images of Tee Tee eating his dick, him hitting her from the back, her swallowing his cum, all popped in his head at once. He felt foul as fuck.

Corey wanted to change the subject. "Them hoes got me on the 6th floor. What floor you on?"

"I'm on the 7th. Damn, I wish we could have at least been on the same floor. I could have told Tee to have one of her homegirls come pull you out for a visit. Or, we could have gone to rec together," Happy told him. They spent the rest of their time together, riding about the world. Soon, the guards came to escort them back to 701.

Eventually, they went their separate ways. Corey was happy to see his cousin, but he was hoping he would never again. The guilt was eating at his soul. While Happy was keeping it all the way solid, Corey was fucking his girl's brains out, slutting her out, every which way he could think of.

Later that evening, Tee went up to the jail to visit Happy. Then, right after, she went to visit Corey. He went ahead and told her where he kept his money stashed. He needed to get a lawyer and would probably need her to handle some things for him. She said she would, and gave him her word she would keep it all the way solid. But, she didn't.

That was the first and last time Tee Tee went to see Corey. She later had her homegirl write him a letter, so the handwriting wouldn't match hers. The letter went on to explain how what they were doing was wrong. And how her conscience wouldn't allow her to continue. She also said she wouldn't be able to come visit him again, and good luck with his situation. Of course, she didn't mention anything about his money.

With no money, Corey wasn't about to fight with a court-appointed. When the State came to him with forty years, he signed. He saw one of Happy's homeboys going to court one day. He told Corey that Happy was taking his case to trial. Corey really hoped he would beat it. He was too real of a nigga to go down like that. Corey asked the same dude about Tee Tee. She was fucking some young nigga. Had him driving Happy's "El Dog". *I guess things never change*, Corey said to himself.

Jaliyah laid curled up on the rancid carpet. Her hands and feet were zip-tied. Gray duct tape covered her lips and eyes. She could smell the stale aroma of wet wood and dry wall. Along with a foul, putrid odor.

She was fearful for her daughter. Up until then, she had no idea if she was dead or alive. She couldn't even fathom the former. She prayed for the hundredth time. For God to deliver her from this evil.

A door creaked open. Jaliyah began to tremble. Ty stood over her and watched with fierce dispassion. Before her was a woman whose only crime was exchanging vows with the man that kidnapped and murdered her precious, sweet, baby boy.

She tilted her head, and studied Jaliyah. Intensely, like a python observing a field mouse that was miraculously dropped into her tank. She and Marcus had agreed to interrogate Jaliyah for information. They still didn't know Pat's whereabouts. The attempt on his life was unsuccessful. Marcus felt Jaliyah was the key to finding out Pat's location. Yeah, Ty *had* agreed.

Now that she was in the same room as the woman, she realized that wouldn't be possible. Armed with a butterfly knife at her side, Ty stalked her prey. As if sensing the impending danger, Jaliyah began to whimper, while trembling. Ty felt nothing for her.

Crouching down beside her, Ty grabbed the woman by the hair and yanked back as hard as she could. "I know you don't know me," she whispered harshly into her ear. "But your husband kidnapped my baby boy. Then, he discarded him like trash." Ty' voice threatened to break, at the mention of CJ.

She steadied her nerves, brought the knife around and placed the tip against her throat. Jaliyah's body shook, as she sobbed for her life. Ty applied pressure. The skin gave way. Then, a soft pop as the blade punctured through her trachea. Jaliyah spasmed. Wet gurgling sounds, muffled by tape.

In and out. In and out. Ty sawed until the bladed kissed her spinal cord. Spouts of blood shot forth like a mini water fountain. Ty tried to saw Jaliyah's spinal cord, but the blade wasn't tough enough to chew through the bone. Giving up, she just stared, as the blood bubbled up and saturated the already filthy carpet. Once she was certain all life was extinguished, Ty stood up and calmly walked out of the room. Devoid of all empathy.

Marcus pulled up to the house, expecting to question Pat's wife. As soon as he stepped foot in the door, he knew something was drastically wrong. Ty had blood all over the knees of her jeans, as well as her forearms. The bloody blade, discarded on the floor next to her. Marcus approached her cautiously. "Ty. Baby. Please tell me you didn't," he whispered. Begging for her to say he was just seeing things. That his concerns were unwarranted. Ty simply just stared up at him. When he looked into her eyes, he knew.

He rushed into the room Jaliyah was being held in. Sure enough, she was laid lifeless on the dirty floor. Her throat was a bloody, mangled, butchered mess. Marcus put his head down. He should have never left Ty in the house alone with her. He saw the signs.

Ever since CJ, Ty had been going further and further into herself. She was constantly throwing up. Her illness already caused her to lose a bunch of weight. Now, she had stopped eating. Ty's once curvaceous body was near skin and bones.

Marcus looked at Jaliyah once more, then shook his head. A sickly thought popped in his head. He sprinted towards the room where baby Jamiyah was being held. Marcus reached for the door knob, closed his eyes and said a quick prayer. He pushed the door open. A great sigh of relief made his body shudder. There, sitting on the floor, playing with her dolls, was baby Jamiyah. Oblivious to the fact, her mother suffered a grisly death, a few feet away.

He was a lot of things, but Marcus wasn't a kid killer. A few months ago, he would have said the same thing about Ty. Now, he wasn't so sure. He knew he had to get Jamiyah out of the house as soon as possible. What to do with her? Where to take her?

The truth of the matter was: there was nowhere else he could take her. The plan was to get the whereabouts of Pat, kill him, then let the wife and kid go. Now that the girl's mother was dead, and the father was soon to be, Marcus felt some type of way about orphaning another child. Having been awarded to the State himself, he didn't want that fate for the little girl.

Then he had an idea. He would ransom her off. Once they get the money, he would return her to her dad. Then he, Ty and Mya could sell the house they got now, and relocate to another state.

Who was he kidding? Ty would never go for that. She didn't have much longer to live. Her mind was set on getting revenge. He decided then, he wouldn't tell her. Hopefully, she would forgive him for the duplicity. He just had to make sure she didn't kill the little girl before he was able to carry out his plan.

Marcus called Chief and asked him to come scoop Ty up and take her home. Chief pulled up in his momma's Jag, twenty minutes later. He saw the state she was in, detached and covered in blood. Marcus confided in Chief about his plan. Chief agreed. Once Ty and Chief were gone, Marcus began to execute. He didn't know where to find Pat. So, he would make Pat look for him.

Pat stood looking at his top crew members. Fuming. Someone made an attempt on his life, *in traffic* and no one knew who. He had his suspicions, but didn't want to make his move until he was certain.

Luckily for him, his bodyguard and driver, Rockz, was a very big man. At 6'5", 295 lbs., he made a very effective shield. When the .762's chewed through the car's frame, Rockz absorbed most of the shots, leaving his insides all over Pat. Besides a few grazes, Pat walked away unscathed. Now, he was seething.

"Shooter. Tell me again, how the fuck did y'all lose them niggas?" Shooter was one of the ones that pursued Marcus and Chief all the way to the East.

"OG. We followed them niggas all the way passed the Budweiser plant. They got off the freeway, and we followed them through Clinton Park. We damn near had them, but it was a trap. They had a group of niggas waiting with sticks to ambush us. Trigger saw the play, just in time. If we would have kept pushing, them niggas would have ate our trucks up."

"So basically, you caught that, pussy," Pat growled, accusingly. Shooter frowned. He respected Pat, but being called a pussy wasn't going to sit well with him. Shooter didn't know how to respond, so he just dropped his head.

"We went there twenty deep. Twenty Motherfucking Niggas! And you mean to tell me, two niggas in a car got the drop on us. I damn near lost my fucking life. And none of you niggas can tell me who's responsible." Spit flew from his mouth, as Pat ranted and raved. "Imma give y'all niggas forty-eight hours to get me some info I can use." When no one moved, he yelled, "What the fuck are y'all waiting for?" They all jumped out of their seats, stumbling over each other in attempts to get out the door.

Pat was left alone, chest heaving, as he struggled to maintain his composure. Honestly, he wanted to cry. He still hadn't heard from his wife and kid. Pat hoped for the best. Deep down, in his subconscious mind, he knew the truth. *I may never see them again.*

He played a couple scenarios in his head. Meme could have sent a couple niggas at him. She must have to know that

Pat was looking for her. He poured himself a shot of Cognac, then sat down in the recliner. He was out of his element. For the last couple years, he'd been in control of his life. Now, it seemed as if his life was utter chaos.

Pat hadn't really been on social media since the situation with Ty's son. *Fuck it!* he thought. He logged on and saw he had multiple messages in DM's. One message intrigued him more than the others. The subject read: *Two Hundred Thousand.*

His heart sped up. He opened up the message. A picture of his daughter popped up. Jamiyah was sitting on a blanket. The room she was in looked devoid of all types of furniture. Pat noticed the user was still online. Pat responded: *??????*

Fifteen seconds later, a response came.

SuddenDeath666: *If u wanna see her again. Two Hundred Thousand in forty-eight hours. If not . . . what's your favorite restaurant?* Pat's hands trembled. He could barely type back.

Pat: *Where?*

SuddenDeath666: *North Channel Park. There's a trail. Come alone, drop the bag and you will get what's yours.*

Pat: *Please. Don't hurt her. Where's my wife?*

He waited for a response. None came. He noticed the *online* light went off. Whoever *SuddenDeath666* was, was no longer connected. He knew he wouldn't go to the authorities, but he wondered if he should have a couple of his homies in position. No, he couldn't risk it. This was his family he was talking about.

Two hundred grand would put a dent in his stash, but he would be far from broke. For his family, he would give up everything he had. He made his mind up. He was going to go to the park one deep and he was going to pay the ransom.

Pat had thirty-four thousand at his duck off, but the bulk of his stash was at the main house. He hadn't been back there since the fiasco with CJ. Then, a thought occurred to him. *What if Jaliyah told them about the safe?* He thought about it. *Naw. They wouldn't be asking for a ransom, if they had access to the stash,* he surmised. Pat grabbed his Glock .40, and went home for the first time in almost a month.

The next night, Meme picked Chief up from his mom's house. They made arrangements to have dinner at *Ruth's Chris,* as well as catching the new Tyler Perry movie.

As they rode in the car, Chief couldn't help but to admire Meme's beauty. Her skin-tight, red Pucci dress made all her curves stand out. He kept staring at her legs as she drove. Fantasizing about having them wrapped around his waist or his head. "Why you keep staring at me like that, boy?" Meme flirted.

"To keep it all the way hot, momma, you bad. I can definitely see myself with you, long term," Chief admitted. This was his first night out with her. But, they'd been conversing on the phone every day since they'd exchanged numbers.

Chief told himself it was all a set up, but if he was being completely honest, he was starting to feel something for her. She was mature, sexy and even though it may be because of the money she stole, she appeared to be banked up. All that was left to be seen was if her sex game was on point.

"Oh, is that right? So now you're trynna trap your very own cougar," she kidded. Meme was definitely feeling the young man also. To be eighteen, he carried himself well. His conversation was surprisingly captivating.

"I wouldn't say *trap.* More like . . . *Entangled,* he finessed. The sexual tension definitely was thick. Each of them fantasized about the other through the night. Once the dinner and movie was over with, they headed to the Scottish Inn, on I-10 and Normandy. For a night cap.

Laura was at home, bored as hell. She sat on the couch, in a red and white, Terry cloth robe. Flipping through the channels. Cindy had her *girlfriend* over, and Laura felt there was too much estrogen in the house. She needed some good, hard dick.

She scrolled through her contacts and came across Meme's name. She smiled. A few hours ago, Meme picked up her son Calvin for their date. Of course, Laura didn't mind that her eighteen-year-old son was messing with a woman almost his mother's age. Who else was better to teach him how to take care of a woman, than a woman.

Laura took a liking to Meme. She reminded the older woman of herself. She felt with the right tutelage, Meme could become a very accomplished woman. Plus, every young man needed at least one older vet to show him the ropes.

Speaking of which, Laura began to think about Marcus and decided to give *her* young stud a call. After two rings, he answered. "Hello?"

"Hey, handsome. What you got planned tonight?"

"Nothing, really. I'm at the spot chilling."

"Well. I was wondering if we could link up tonight. I need some of that good, young cock in my life," she purred.

Marcus got quiet. Ever since that situation with Ty and Jaliyah, he'd been at the hideout, supervising little Jamiyah. He would have to relocate the child, but he honestly didn't have anywhere else to take her.

The house smelled like death. Justifiably so. He had only one more day. Everything was riding on Pat's love for his family. The meet up was for tomorrow night. *I can afford to blow off some steam,"* he reasoned. *Little Jamiyah will be safe for a couple hours.*

"That's a bet, but I can't stay long. I'll be at your crib in thirty minutes."

"No. Not here," she corrected him. She didn't need Cindy all up in her mix. "Meet me at the Scottish Inn, off I-10 and Normandy."

"A'ight. Well, I'll be there. Just let me get myself together real quick." Marcus hung the phone up, then peeked in on little Jamiyah. She was sound asleep. Bundled up. Laying on the floor, with her Barbie clutched against her chest. Marcus knew he shouldn't leave her by herself, but figured he wouldn't be long. He closed the door, hopped in Ty's car and headed back to the East.

Ty sat in the back seat of an Uber. An older African American woman with dreads and facial piercings drove her to her destination. She couldn't believe Marcus had her sent home. Like she was a child.

She killed Pat's wife . . . and so what? The bitch deserved to die. If Pat wasn't hiding like a little bitch, she would have done him in too. "*Aghuu Aghuu.*" Ty coughed into a handkerchief. Globs of blood and phlegm materialized. It had been almost a year since the doctor diagnosed her. They told her six to eight months. She was in *overtime* right now.

She'd been going so hard for her kids that she barely noticed how sick she was. It wasn't until CJ died. That's when she really started to feel it. *At least I'll be able to leave something behind for Mya,* she thought. Not long after being picked up, the Uber stopped at the location.

Ty wondered if the Uber driver could feel what awaited in that old and decrepit house. Probably not. Many houses on the street were affected by the storm. When she stepped out of the vehicle, the distinct stench of rotting, molded wood, assaulted her nostrils. Ty caught a whiff of a more sinister scent, and smiled. She noticed her car was gone. *Marcus isn't here,* she smiled to herself.

Ty waited for the Uber driver to turn off the street, brake lights disappearing into the night, before making her way up the walkway. She stepped into the house. The putrid smell of decaying flesh was now starting to ripen. She lurched towards the room Jamiyah was kept in.

Ty opened the door slowly. Baby Jamiyah was asleep, peacefully on the floor. Oblivious to what type of evil stirred in the grown woman's heart. *I remember when CJ was that small,* Ty thought, as she stepped further into the room. Even though no one else was in the house, she closed the door behind her.

Chapter 15

'*Slurp. Slurp. Slurp. Sluurrrrpppp.*' "Mmmmh." Meme moaned around Chief's dick, as he continued to grudge-fuck her face. They'd been going at it since they stepped foot in the motel room. This was already round number three. The way it was looking, it would be an all-night affair.

Chief reached over and peeled her bright, yellow ass cheeks apart. Her pink pussy continued to drool all over the cheap, bed spread. He slid his middle finger into her snatch, dug with it a few times, then pulled it out. Right before he pushed it into her asshole.

Meme tensed up for the slightest moment, then relaxed. She grunted around his dick, as he fucked her booty hole with his longest digit. So far, they'd performed almost every position. Now, it was time to see what that ole dookie shoot was about. Meme felt—knew—what was coming. Her mouth seemed to get wetter. '*SMACK!*'

Her ass cheek clapped as Chief gave her a hard smack. "Lay on your back." She scrambled to get in position. Chief grabbed a pillow, then placed it under her ass. Leaving her elevated and at his mercy. He brought her legs together. "Hold them closed."

Meme wrapped her arms around the crook of her knees and pulled her legs all the way back. The same way Olympic divers do, when they're flipping into the pool. Her knee caps pressed against her breasts. Her pussy popped out, lips splayed open.

Chief sat in position. He grabbed his rod at the base and dipped it into the mouth of her pussy. Her walls snapped at his helmet, eager to swallow his cock whole. He pulled out and let the tip rest at the center of her anal ring. With his left thumb, he peeled the hood of her clit back. Exposing, and massaging her button, while at the same time driving through a barrier.

A soft "pop" and increase in pressure let him know he'd broken the seal. He looked down. What a wonderful sight. Her mud flaps grabbed at his dick, as he began to saw in and out. To her credit, she took it like a champ.

Never once did she beg him to stop, or tell him to ease up. She let the young nigga fuck her asshole, as if he owned it. Not long after, Chief's nuts began to ache. That oh-so-familiar tingle began to work its way up. From his toes to his sack. "Fuck . . . Sssshit, Meme. This ass is so fucking tight . . . Damn, bitch. You finna make me cum."

"Cum in my ass, baby. Fill that booty hole up." Chief gripped the backs of her thighs, tilted his head back and roared.

"Aggghhhh . . . Fuuucccckkk!" His dick jerked and spat out globs of hot dick milk. Filling her rim to the brim. Meme's ass muscles clenched, clutched and choked at his cock. It felt like a vice grip over his shaft. He collapsed next to her, panting.

She was definitely everything he was hoping for. Meme's wet pussy blew his mind. It seemed as though there was nothing she wouldn't let him do. Too exhausted to get up and take a shower yet, they decided to blow a blunt.

As they smoked, loud banging could be heard through the wall next door. Then came the muffled cries of a woman getting royally fucked. Even though the words were distorted, you could still hear her lustful pleas. "Oh my gawd. Fuck me deep in my ass." Then moments later. "Cum in my mouth, baby. I want you to fill momma's tummy up. Let me eat that nut."

Hearing the couple next door had Chief primed and ready to go another round. *Whoever that nigga is, he's killing that bitch's pussy,* Chief thought to himself. He couldn't let dude outshine him like that. Chief climbed back on top of Meme. "One more for the road," he whispered to her, as he sank to the bottom of her hot box.

Marcus pulled his slimy cock out of Laura's ass, and shoved it straight into her mouth. Without hesitation, she sucked, slurped, and swallowed until he was a trembling mess. Nuts emptied and shaft was shining. *That's* why he couldn't get enough of her. Her sex game was off the chain. She would let him do *literally* whatever he wanted to her body.

Yet, he knew this had to be the last time. Not because of her, but because of Chief. That was his ace nigga, and he knew if Chief were to ever find out . . . World War 3. Justifiably so. Two things you don't do: Fuck your best friend's girl or his mom.

As he looked down at his dick, sliding in and out of her soft, pillowy lips, Marcus felt sad. He did not want to stop messing with her, but he had to make this the last time. *Imma break it to her afterwards,* he told himself.

He heard the headboard knocking next door. The couple in the next room had been going at it, longer than Laura and Marcus had. Whoever they were, had him and Laura riled up. It seemed as if they were each competing with each other.

Less than an hour later, after a quick shower, they were ready to leave. He watched Laura throw on her sundress, no panties and couldn't do anything else but shake his head. Leaving her alone would be one of the hardest things he ever had to do.

Laura caught him staring. She smiled. "Boy. Why you looking at me like that?"

"Like what?"

"I don't know." Laura replied. "Like you're scared of me or something."

"Naw. I'm just doing some heavy thinking. My mind's just spinning right now," he told her.

"Well, baby, don't think too hard. Sometimes, it's better to just go with the flow," she said, as they headed out the room. At that exact same moment, the couple next door was leaving their room also.

The first person Marcus saw was Meme. He instinctively reached for his waist. Nothing there. At Laura's insistence, he'd left his strap in the car.

Suddenly Marcus's companion walked out of the room, and Chief's jaw dropped. "Marcus . . . *Momma?*" Meme looked at Marcus, then at Laura. Bewildered, she had no idea the mother and son knew Marcus. Then, the realization hit. Marcus was the one blowing the woman's back out. And the woman was Laura, Chief's mom.

Before he knew what he was doing, his face contorted, Chief pulled his Glock off his waists and upped it on Marcus. "Nigga. You fucking my momma?"

Marcus threw his hands up. "Chief . . . Hold up, bro . . . Let's talk 'bout this."

"I don't wanna talk, bitch ass nigga. I trusted you, and you do some foul shit like this?" Marcus saw the look in his eyes. He knew his best friend better than anyone, besides the woman standing next to him. The woman he'd just got done fucking.

He had two choices. One. Try and make it to his pole. But knowing Chief, if he felt Marcus was headed for a gun, Marcus would never make it to his car. Two. Try and disarm him. Considering they were three to four feet apart, he figured he may have a chance at that. Marcus focused on the barrel, as Chief continued to scream his outrage, Laura frantically begged her son to drop the weapon.

Marcus's heart thundered in his chest. He glanced at Meme. Shock, confusion and fear, plastered on her face.

Chief's grip tightened around the gun handle. His index finger flirted with the trigger. *It's now or never.*

Quick as a viper, Marcus lunged forward. *'Bocka. Bocka.'* Two quick shots rang out. The first caught Marcus in the shoulder, causing him to spin at a downward angle. The second connected with the side of his head. Crushing his temple. His body went limp, mid fall.

He landed with a sick thud. Dead before his body hit the ground. "Oh my God. Oh my God, Calvin, what have you done?" Laura screamed. She dropped to her knees, shaking Marcus, as if he was just merely taking a nap. A pool of blood, two feet in diameter, formed beneath him. The strong scent of iron polluted the air. Chief snapped out of his rage.

Eyes wide, hands trembling, he spoke. "I didn't mean to. I swear to God, I didn't mean to. *FUCK!*" He screamed in frustration.

Laura's motherly instincts kicked in. "You need to get the hell out of here. Now, Calvin!" Chief looked around for Meme. She'd vanished. He scanned the parking lot. Her car was gone. Chief took one more look at his best friend, dead with his brains all over the concrete, and took off running down the street.

He made it down the road. Police sirens could be heard blaring in the distance. Chief needed to find somewhere to hide his pistol. He came across a dumpster, and tossed it in. His mind was racing. So was his heart. Even though he was pissed as hell, hurt at the betrayal, he didn't want Marcus to die. *Why the fuck did he try and rush me?* Chief kept asking himself.

He was about twenty minutes away from his mom's house. Add to that, he couldn't take any of the back roads. So, the journey would take even longer.

By the time he made it home, he was drenched in sweat. Laura still hadn't made it back. He debated calling her cell phone, but didn't want her to answer while she was around the police. All he could do was wait.

Chief hopped in the shower. While the water washed away the tears and dirt, the guilt would be something he could never get rid of.

It's the night of the drop. Pat had been on social media all day, trying to connect with *SuddenDeath666*. No response. He sat in his living room, draped in all black. Staring at the duffle bag, filled with enough money to change a broke nigga's life. Just over a month ago, he was the one asking for a ransom. Now. He couldn't think about that. Reason being, the last kidnapping didn't go too well for the kidnappee.

Pat's leg wouldn't sit still. His nerves were fried. He checked his buss down Cartier once again. Even though he hadn't heard from the kidnappers all day, he already had the time and the place. He grabbed the bag, his P90 and headed out the door.

When Pat pulled up to North Channel Park, it was completely deserted. Not long ago, there was a story about a man found dead. Just sitting in the car, while the kids played soccer in the field, twenty yards away.

Pat parked his 600 Benz, in that exact same parking spot. He waited. Constantly checking his Instagram. *Nothing!* Finally, he said to hell with it, hopped out the car with the bag. After placing it down in the trail, Pat headed back to his car and waited.

Thirty minutes passed the agreed upon time. Then, an hour. After three and a half hours, Pat went to retrieve the money. He still didn't want to leave just yet. *Maybe they're just running late,* he guessed. So, he waited another two hours. Daylight began to peek its head over the cover of darkness. Pat begrudgingly put his Benz in drive, and headed back home. Heart heavy with sorrow and worry.

Corey arrived on the Estelle unit, and couldn't be any more satisfied. Estelle was known for two things. Sick inmates and beautiful female guards. He wasn't sick, so the game God must have shot him a blessing.

A week after he'd arrived, he bumped into one of his free world niggas. A cat by the name of G-Mack. Mack had been sentenced to thirty years for a robbery, seven years prior. Of course, when Corey saw him, he couldn't contain his excitement. He was happy to be on the unit with someone he actually knew from the world.

G-Mack showed him the ropes. Laced him up on which guards were *for the game*, and which ones he needed to stay clear of. Of course, G-Mack had a female guard on his team named Flernoy. A slim, yellow thing, with long hair and a nice juicy bubble butt. Corey even held jiggers, while G-Mack fucked her in the utility closet.

One day, they were leaving the barbershop when someone caught Corey's attention. An inmate in a wheelchair was getting pushed into the infirmary by another inmate. He looked very familiar to Corey. *It couldn't be,* Corey doubted.

He tapped Mack on the arm. "Say. Did you see that nigga in that wheelchair that just passed us up?"

"Yeah. Wassup?"

"He looked familiar. Do you know who it was?"

"Yeah. That's Bo. He from the hood. He was fucking with Ty when I left the world," G- Mack told him.

Corey began to chuckle lightly. "Maannn, gone on. I know dude. I was fucking his bitch."

G-Mack looked surprised. "Yeah. You talkin' bout Ty?" Corey nodded. "She got some good?"

"What? Hell yeah. Pussy A-1. Head game, the truth. She gon' let a nigga put that dick anywhere he want to. And, she gon' take it like a gangsta. Stone-cold freak. I was fucking her and her best friend Meme." Corey paused. He wasn't sure if he should continue, but did anyway. "To keep it all the way a buck, the murder case he got is really mine. That nigga ain't do shit, but the white folks still slammed his ass."

"Damn." G-Mack shook his head.

"What happened to him?" Corey asked.

"Oh. Maann, dude out of there. He's been down here playing in that mud," G-Mack alerted him. Now it was Corey's turn to be surprised.

"G, you're bullshitting. Bo?"

"Facts, my G. He was on the Ferg. They say one of the punks he was fucking with had a boyfriend. The nigga supposedly hit him up in the showers. The nigga did him dirty too. The blade nicked his spine. That's why he's in the chair. But, that ain't the worst part. Come to find out, bro got HIV."

Corey's jaw hit the ground. *Did he have it before he came to jail? How long does it take to show up in your blood?* Corey's mind wouldn't stop spinning with questions.

G-Mack must have sensed his unease. "You good. They say he caught it while he was fucking with that punk on the Ferg named Rose. Supposedly, they segged the punk. He got a bunch of them niggas over there sick."

Corey kept shaking his head in disbelief. Even though he and Bo weren't friends, he would've never thought he would go out like that. Bo had always been a thorough, street nigga. His gun game was adequate, but his knuckle game was legendary.

As they passed up the infirmary, Corey couldn't resist looking inside. Sure enough, it *was* Bo. "That's crazy," is all he could say, as he shook his head. He and G-Mack continued down the hallway.

A week after Marcus was shot and killed, authorities received a tip to search a condemned house in the Greenspoint area. Three bodies were found. The only saving grace: little Jamiyah's body wasn't mutilated, like her mom's or her big cousin's.

Forensics had determined the toddler had been strangled to death. Police were aggressively looking for clues. So was Pat. Since the discovery, Pat had been on rampage.

Ty had been wise enough to pull Mya out of North Shore. She sent her to go live with some relatives out of town. Pat didn't have anything else to live for. The money. His jewels. His freedom. All of it meant nothing. Not without a family there to enjoy it with.

After a week of tearing the city up, he finally took a break to finish organizing the funeral. Pat spared no expense. He told himself, the two hundred thousand he was willing to pay for the ransom would be spent to send off his loved ones. Three of the most important people in his life were gone.

Gold trimmed caskets. Thousands of roses were ordered. Three processions paraded through the city. Pat sat sulking in a sleek, black Escalade limo. At the protest of his lieutenants, he chose to be left alone. Just him and a bottle of Hennessy. Tears streaked down his grief-stricken face, as he reminisced.

His phone rang. He checked the caller ID. *His great aunt Alice.* "Hey, Auntie."

"Hey, Pooh Pooh . . . Where you at?" Hearing his aunt refer to him by his old family nickname made Pat smile.

"I'm almost there. Is everybody waiting on me?" he slurred, obviously drunk out of his mind.

"Of course we are. We're always waiting on you. Now, get your butt down here," she ordered.

"Yes, ma'am," Pat conceded, before hanging the phone up.

Minutes later, he arrived at the cemetery. The service was beautiful. There were so many people there, Pat didn't recognize half the faces. Once he arrived, the service began.

Pat cried for each of them. But, when it was time to celebrate his princess, he shattered. She was so innocent. She didn't have an evil bone in her body. She was the same little girl that begged her daddy to keep a frog because it hurt its leg. And someone took her life. Just to spite Pat.

Through all his grief and sorrow, he had yet to come to the realization that maybe *this* was what CJ's family went through. Somewhere in his mind, he rationalized. *CJ's death had been a necessity. A debt had to be repaid.*

As he stood there, watching his baby girl's casket being lowered into the dirt, something caught his eye. If he would've been on point, he probably would've thought to make sure everyone in his circumference were family and close friends.

With so many well-wishers, he didn't notice. One of the hearse drivers looked, oh, so familiar. She must've been wearing padding underneath her uniform.

Ty looked to be twenty pounds heavier. Her hat covered most of her blond wig. *If* he had been sober, he'd have seen it a mile away. Be that as it may, he was falling down, pissy drunk.

He hadn't realized that Ty had infiltrated the sacred event, and had a gun pointed at his head. Until she was two feet away! "For CJ," she firmly said, before squeezing. *'Bocka. Bocka.'* Red mist exploded from Pat's cranium. His head snapped. His body jerked, falling to the ground like a sack of potatoes.

Screams began to rise. Women yelled obscenities. Men, particularly crew members, rushed to grab their weapons. Ty neither feared, nor ran. She arrived, knowing full well what was needed of her. She stood over Pat's lifeless body, spat, aimed and fired. *'Bocka. Bocka. Bocka.'* Three more hollow tips riddled his corpse.

Tears poured down her cheeks. She looked to the heavens. "Momma's coming, baby. Tell Marcus, momma's on the way." *'Bocka. Bocka. Bocka. Bocka.'* Ty jerked, as searing, hot metal bore through her body. Before she knew what was going on, she was laying on the ground. She tried to breathe. It was as if she was underwater.

Pat's men approached her timidly. Guns up and at the ready. Blood poured from her mouth. Her teeth were stained, dark red. She laid on the ground twitching. Her jaw began to chatter. An immense cold enveloped her being. She mustered all the strength she had left, in an attempt to pick up the gun, aim and shoot.

'Bocka. Bocka. Bocka. Bocka.' The group of men unloaded their weapons. Ty's body became riddled with bullets. The firing ceased only when guns could be heard clicking on *empty*. Ty laid breathless, eyes wide, bloody smile on her face.

Mya had just left the Estelle unit, visiting her dad. This was the first time she'd had an opportunity to go see him. She was shocked he was in a wheelchair. When asked what happened, he simply said it was a freak accident. That he would tell her about it some other time.

She debated on whether or not she should tell him *all* of what transpired, since he'd been gone. In the end, she felt he deserved to know.

Mya still couldn't believe she was out there on her own. Well, technically not. She was staying with her aunt, Delores, in Conroe. But, everyone in her immediate family was either dead or in jail. The only thing she had to her name was the house her mom and Marcus left her.

She would forever be grateful to them for that. With the help of her aunt, Delores, Mya had been renting the house out. The lease was $1,300 a month. For a girl still in school, that wasn't bad at all.

Chief reached out to her, once he got arrested and booked in for murder. She was going to ride it out with him, until she found out *who* he killed. Mya immediately stopped answering his phone calls.

She'd inherited her mother's trusty, old Malibu. As she drove down 45 south, back to Houston, tears began to fall down her face. She was just lucky to be alive. So much death around her.

A few days later, Mya was shopping when someone vaguely familiar approached her. "Excuse me. I don't mean to bother you, but by any chance, would you happen to be the daughter of Tynesha Jackson?"

Mya was stunned but also leery. Her mom had messed over so many people before she died, she didn't know what type of timing someone would be on when they asked about her mother. "Yes. She *was* my mother."

The man picked up on the innuendo. "Did something happen to her?"

"She passed away," Mya replied. The man looked surprised, then thought about it.

"If you don't mind me asking, how?" Mya didn't know what type of angle the man was playing. But, she decided to play along.

"Gunshot wound." He almost looked relieved. "Oh. I'm sorry. I'm Doctor Jordan. Almost a year ago, your mother had been admitted to East Houston Medical Center. After initial test and blood work, our staff determined *prematurely*, that your mother suffered from Lupus as well as Pancreatic Cancer. Now, the Lupus was a correct diagnosis, but the cancer was a false read. Due to the existence of the Lupus and a mix up of her charts, we gave your mother a death date she didn't deserve. We tried to reach her, but her phone was off, and no one resided at the address she gave us."

Mya's knees buckled. The last months of her life, her mother lived them the way she did because she assumed she was about to die anyway. If she had known she had a full life ahead of her, Ty would have led her life differently. The doctor apologized once again, before leaving Mya with her thoughts. The rest of the day, Mya tortured herself with a thousand different "what ifs."

Bo wheeled himself back to his cell. Tears continued to pour down his face, falling into his lap. He no longer cared about wiping them away. The first time his daughter comes to see him, she drops a bomb on him. His family's no more.

Mya tried to spare him the gruesome details, but Bo wouldn't have it. He wanted every single one.

He especially sobbed when he heard what happened to Junior. Bo felt like a failure. As a man, the protector of his household, he let his family down. Even though he was innocent of all the charges levied against him, that didn't change the fact. Bo wasn't there when they most needed him.

Now, he was a shell of his former self. After the attempt on his life, he'd been rushed to intensive care surgery. His intestines had been ripped to shreds. In order for him to be able to process food, surgeons had to go in and cut large portions of his intestines out.

His bowel movements were now sporadic. He was forced to wear an adult diaper. The humiliation was trumped by the fact he had been diagnosed with HIV. Apparently, Rose was infected.

Bo's life had so much promise. But, because of his lack of discipline and his disregard for principles, he deprived his body of a fighting chance. Even though HIV was no longer a death sentence, it still wreaked havoc on the human body. There was still no cure. Bo would spend the rest of his life suffering. With the less than adequate care provided, that suffering would only become exponential.

He sat in his single man cell, sorrow and grief laying heavy on his soul. So heavy, you could almost hear the line swinging, then *snap.* With trembling hands, Bo reached for his bedsheet.

He reminisced about the first time he and Ty made love. The tenderness, until finally she begged for that savage shit. The first steps Mya took, then CJ's first words. *Da Da.*

Bo sobbed uncontrollably, as he secured the sheet though the top locker. He wrapped the other end around his neck, making sure it was secure. He was never one to believe in God, or the afterlife, but lately he'd been praying. He said a prayer then.

Not for him, but for his daughter, praying she may find the strength to forgive him for what he was about to do. The perseverance to be able to move on and make something of her life.

With the sheet wrapped securely around his neck, Bo propelled himself out of the wheelchair. The slack tightened. The veins in his neck bulged. His vision became spotty. His chest felt like it was about to explode. There in his cell, right after his daughter came to visit him, Chadwick Bowman Sr. took his own life.

One Year Later—
She kept up with the gossip. Who got killed and what not. But to venture back to the East. *Better not!* Meme took another sip of her drink. Eyeing the scene of the club, over the rim of her glass.

Since that dreadful night at the Scottish Inn, Meme hadn't been back to the East. She changed her number, and moved to a whole other city. *Conroe Texas.* Even though it was a whole hell of a lot slower, it was also safer.

She desperately needed to find a benefactor. The money she stole from Ty had basically dwindled down to almost nothing. She watched the young crowd, and couldn't help but think about Chief. She wondered. Was he feeling her for real, or was it all a set up? Did Laura know about her taking the money from Ty? Even though she admired the older woman, she cut off all communication with her also.

One thing she couldn't question about Chief, though. That boy's dick game was astounding. Because of him, she turned out on that young meat.

Meme saw the news. Ty went out like a suicide Taliban member. She had to tilt her hat, though. Meme asked herself. *If the shoe was on the other foot, would I be able to wipe out Pat's whole family?* Setting up *CJ to get kidnapped was one thing, but could I actually, physically kill a child? . . . No way!*

She continued to watch the crowd. She might be the oldest woman in the spot. Even though the club was eighteen and up, most patrons weren't over twenty-eight. Still, she wasn't to be ignored.

With a short, black, see-through Valentino dress, no bra and a black G-string, every heterosexual dick in the club was at attention. But Meme wasn't looking for just any dick. She was searching for *that* right one.

A young nigga about his bag. One she could groom and mold. One she could wrap around her finger, as her lips wrap around his cock. This was the third weekend, and she still hadn't found him yet. Feeling frustrated, she decided to leave and see if she could find another watering hole.

As she walked outside, the cool breeze caressed her face. Her nipples hardened. Her four-inch Botega heels click-clacked against the gravel, as she strutted to her Jaguar. Meme reached for the door handle and a sudden panic took hold of her.

She felt a presence, nanoseconds before the gloved hand wrapped around her mouth. Before the pinching. Then the blade, sawing in and out of her insides. Her attacker's grip was solid and true. Try as she might, Meme couldn't escape their grasp. As her life's blood left her body, so did her strength.

Her knees gave out. The attacker allowed her to sink onto the pavement. Once they saw Meme had seconds before her light was extinguished, they leaned over and whispered in her ear. "That was for CJ. You dirty bitch."

Meme's eyes bucked with recognition. Her lungs flooded with blood. *It couldn't be. How did she find me?* was the last thought she had in this world. The last thing she saw? The back of her *niece* walking off into the night.

The End

Lock Down Publications and Ca$h Presents
Assisted Publishing Packages

Due to an increase in the price of services we have increased our prices. The prices below reflect the price increase as of 11/1/24.

BASIC PACKAGE	UPGRADED PACKAGE
$699	$1000
Editing	Typing
Cover Design	Editing
Formatting	Cover Design
	Formatting
	Upload eBooks to Amazon
	Upload Paperback to Amazon
ADVANCE PACKAGE	**LDP SUPREME PACKAGE**
$1,400	$1,700
Typing	Typing
Editing (line editing/content)	Editing (line editing/content)
Cover Design	Cover Design
Formatting	Formatting
Copyright Registration	Copyright Registration
Proofreading	Proofreading
Upload eBooks to Amazon	Set up Amazon Account
Upload Paperback to Amazon	Upload eBooks to Amazon
	Upload Paperback to Amazon
	Advertise on LDP's Amazon and Facebook Page

***Other services available upon request.
Additional charges may apply

Lock Down Publications
P.O. Box 944
Stockbridge, GA 30281-9998
Phone: 470 303-9761
Email: lockdownpublications@gmail.com

Submission Guideline

Submit the first three chapters of your completed manuscript to ldpsubmissions@gmail.com. In the subject line add **Your Book's Title**. The manuscript must be in a Word Doc file and sent as an attachment. Document should be in Times New Roman, double spaced, and in size 12 font. Also, provide your synopsis and full contact information. If sending multiple submissions, they must each be in a separate email.

Have a story but no way to send it electronically? You can still submit to LDP/Ca$h Presents. Send in the first three chapters, written or typed, of your completed manuscript to:

LDP: Submissions Dept
P.O. Box 944
Stockbridge, GA 30281-9998

DO NOT send original manuscript. Must be a duplicate. Provide your synopsis and a cover letter containing your full contact information.

Thanks for considering LDP and Ca$h Presents.

NEW RELEASES

BLOODLINE OF A SAVAGE 1&2
THESE VICIOUS STREETS 1&2
RELENTLESS GOON
RELENTLESS GOON 2
BY PRINCE A. TAUHID

THE BUTTERFLY MAFIA 1-3
BY FUMIYA PAYNE

A THUG'S STREET PRINCESS 1&2
BY MEESHA

CITY OF SMOKE 2
BY MOLOTTI

STEPPERS 1,2&3
THE REAL BADDIES OF CHI-RAQ
BY KING RIO

THE LANE 1&2
BY KEN-KEN SPENCE

THUG OF SPADES 1&2
LOVE IN THE TRENCHES 2
CORNER BOYS
BY COREY ROBINSON

TIL DEATH 3
BY ARYANNA

THE BIRTH OF A GANGSTER 4
BY DELMONT PLAYER

PRODUCT OF THE STREETS 1&2
BY DEMOND "MONEY" ANDERSON

NO TIME FOR ERROR
BY KEESE

MONEY HUNGRY DEMONS
BY TRANAY ADAMS

Coming Soon from Lock Down Publications/Ca$h Presents

IF YOU CROSS ME ONCE 6
ANGEL V
By Anthony Fields

IMMA DIE BOUT MINE 5
By Aryanna

A THUGS STREET PRINCESS 3
By Meesha

PRODUCT OF THE STREETS 3
By Demond Money Anderson

CORNER BOYS 2
By Corey Robinson

THE MURDER QUEENS 6&7
By Michael Gallon

CITY OF SMOKE 3
By Molotti

CONFESSIONS OF A DOPE BOY
By Nicholas Lock

THA TAKEOVER
By Keith Chandler

BETRAYAL OF A G 2
By Ray Vinci

CRIME BOSS
By Playa Ray

Available Now

RESTRAINING ORDER 1 & 2
By **CA$H & Coffee**

LOVE KNOWS NO BOUNDARIES 1-3
By **Coffee**

RAISED AS A GOON I, II, III & IV
BRED BY THE SLUMS I, II, III
BLAST FOR ME I & II
ROTTEN TO THE CORE I II III
A BRONX TALE I, II, III
DUFFLE BAG CARTEL I II III IV V VI
HEARTLESS GOON I II III IV V
A SAVAGE DOPEBOY I II
DRUG LORDS I II III
CUTTHROAT MAFIA I II
KING OF THE TRENCHES
By **Ghost**

LAY IT DOWN I & II
LAST OF A DYING BREED I II
BLOOD STAINS OF A SHOTTA I & II III
By **Jamaica**

LOYAL TO THE GAME I II III
LIFE OF SIN I, II III
By **TJ & Jelissa**

IF LOVING HIM IS WRONG…I & II
LOVE ME EVEN WHEN IT HURTS I II III
By **Jelissa**

PUSH IT TO THE LIMIT
By **Bre' Hayes**

COUNTDOWN OF A KILLA 2 | LO-LIFE

BLOODY COMMAS I & II
SKI MASK CARTEL I, II & III
KING OF NEW YORK I II, III IV V
RISE TO POWER I II III
COKE KINGS I II III IV V
BORN HEARTLESS I II III IV
KING OF THE TRAP I II
By **T.J. Edwards**

WHEN THE STREETS CLAP BACK I & II III
THE HEART OF A SAVAGE I II III IV
MONEY MAFIA I II
LOYAL TO THE SOIL I II III
By **Jibril Williams**

A DISTINGUISHED THUG STOLE MY HEART I II & III
LOVE SHOULDN'T HURT I II III IV
RENEGADE BOYS 1-4
PAID IN KARMA 1-3
SAVAGE STORMS 1-3
AN UNFORESEEN LOVE 1-3
BABY, I'M WINTERTIME COLD 1-3
A THUG'S STREET PRINCESS 1&2
By **Meesha**

A GANGSTER'S CODE 1-3
A GANGSTER'S SYN 1-3
THE SAVAGE LIFE 1-3
CHAINED TO THE STREETS 1-3
BLOOD ON THE MONEY 1-3
A GANGSTA'S PAIN 1-3
BEAUTIFUL LIES AND UGLY TRUTHS
CHURCH IN THESE STREETS
By **J-Blunt**

CUM FOR ME 1-8
An LDP Erotica Collaboration

BLOOD OF A BOSS 1-5
SHADOWS OF THE GAME
TRAP BASTARD
By **Askari**

THE STREETS BLEED MURDER 1-3
THE HEART OF A GANGSTA 1-3
By **Jerry Jackson**

WHEN A GOOD GIRL GOES BAD
By **Adrienne**

THE COST OF LOYALTY 1-3
By **Kweli**

BRIDE OF A HUSTLA 1-3
THE FETTI GIRLS 1-3
CORRUPTED BY A GANGSTA 1-4
BLINDED BY HIS LOVE
THE PRICE YOU PAY FOR LOVE 1-3
DOPE GIRL MAGIC 1-3
By **Destiny Skai**

A KINGPIN'S AMBITION
A KINGPIN'S AMBITION II
I MURDER FOR THE DOUGH
By **Ambitious**

TRUE SAVAGE 1-7
DOPE BOY MAGIC 1-3
MIDNIGHT CARTEL 1-3
CITY OF KINGZ 1&2
NIGHTMARE ON SILENT AVE
THE PLUG OF LIL MEXICO 1&2
CLASSIC CITY
By **Chris Green**

LOVE & CHASIN' PAPER
By **Qay Crockett**

TO DIE IN VAIN
SINS OF A HUSTLA
By **ASAD**

BROOKLYN HUSTLAZ
By **Boogsy Morina**

BROOKLYN ON LOCK 1 & 2
By **Sonovia**

GANGSTA CITY
By **Teddy Duke**

A DRUG KING AND HIS DIAMOND 1-3
A DOPEMAN'S RICHES
HER MAN, MINE'S TOO 1&2
CASH MONEY HO'S
THE WIFEY I USED TO BE 1&2
PRETTY GIRLS DO NASTY THINGS
By **Nicole Goosby**

LIPSTICK KILLAH 1-3
CRIME OF PASSION 1-3
FRIEND OR FOE 1-3
By **Mimi**

TRAPHOUSE KING 1-3
KINGPIN KILLAZ 1-3
STREET KINGS 1&2
PAID IN BLOOD 1&2
CARTEL KILLAZ 1-3
DOPE GODS 1&2
By **Hood Rich**

THE STREETS ARE CALLING
By **Duquie Wilson**

STEADY MOBBN' 1-3
THE STREETS STAINED MY SOUL 1-3
By **Marcellus Allen**

WHO SHOT YA 1-3
SON OF A DOPE FIEND 1-4
HEAVEN GOT A GHETTO 1&2
SKI MASK MONEY 1&2
By **Renta**

GORILLAZ IN THE BAY 1-4
TEARS OF A GANGSTA 1/&2
3X KRAZY 1&2
STRAIGHT BEAST MODE 1&2
By **DE'KARI**

TRIGGADALE 1-3
MURDA WAS THE CASE 1-3
By **Elijah R. Freeman**

SLAUGHTER GANG 1-3
RUTHLESS HEART 1-3
By **Willie Slaughter**

GOD BLESS THE TRAPPERS 1-3
THESE SCANDALOUS STREETS 1-3
FEAR MY GANGSTA 1-5
THESE STREETS DON'T LOVE NOBODY 1-2
BURY ME A G 1-5
A GANGSTA'S EMPIRE 1-4
THE DOPEMAN'S BODYGAURD 1&2
THE REALEST KILLAZ 1-3
THE LAST OF THE OGS 1-3
By **Tranay Adams**

MARRIED TO A BOSS 1-3
By **Destiny Skai & Chris Green**

KINGZ OF THE GAME 1-7
CRIME BOSS 1-3
By **Playa Ray**

FUK SHYT
By **Blakk Diamond**

DON'T F#CK WITH MY HEART 1&2
By **Linnea**

ADDICTED TO THE DRAMA 1-3
IN THE ARM OF HIS BOSS
By **Jamila**

LOYALTY AIN'T PROMISED 1&2
By **Keith Williams**

YAYO 1-4
A SHOOTER'S AMBITION 1&2
BRED IN THE GAME
By **S. Allen**

TRAP GOD 1-3
RICH $AVAGE 1-3
MONEY IN THE GRAVE 1-3
CARTEL MONEY
By **Martell Troublesome Bolden**

FOREVER GANGSTA 1&2
GLOCKS ON SATIN SHEETS 1&2
By **Adrian Dulan**

TOE TAGZ 1-4
LEVELS TO THIS SHYT 1&2
IT'S JUST ME AND YOU
By **Ah'Million**

COUNTDOWN OF A KILLA 2 | LO-LIFE

KINGPIN DREAMS 1-3
RAN OFF ON DA PLUG
By **Paper Boi Rari**

THE STREETS MADE ME 1-3
By **Larry D. Wright**

CONFESSIONS OF A GANGSTA 1-4
CONFESSIONS OF A JACKBOY 1-3
CONFESSIONS OF A HITMAN
By **Nicholas Lock**

I'M NOTHING WITHOUT HIS LOVE
SINS OF A THUG
TO THE THUG I LOVED BEFORE
A GANGSTA SAVED XMAS
IN A HUSTLER I TRUST
By **Monet Dragun**

QUIET MONEY 1-3
THUG LIFE 1-3
EXTENDED CLIP 1&2
A GANGSTA'S PARADISE
By **Trai'Quan**

CAUGHT UP IN THE LIFE 1-3
THE STREETS NEVER LET GO 1-3
By **Robert Baptiste**

NEW TO THE GAME 1-3
MONEY, MURDER & MEMORIES 1-3
By **Malik D. Rice**

CREAM 2-3
THE STREETS WILL TALK
By **Yolanda Moore**

THE STREETS WILL NEVER CLOSE 1-3
By **K'ajji**

LIFE OF A SAVAGE 1-4
A GANGSTA'S QUR'AN 1-4
MURDA SEASON 1-3
GANGLAND CARTEL 1-3
CHI'RAQ GANGSTAS 1-4
KILLERS ON ELM STREET 1-3
JACK BOYZ N DA BRONX 1-3
A DOPEBOY'S DREAM 1-3
JACK BOYS VS DOPE BOYS 1-3
COKE GIRLZ
COKE BOYS
SOSA GANG 1&2
BRONX SAVAGES
BODYMORE KINGPINS
BLOOD OF A GOON
By **Romell Tukes**

CONCRETE KILLA 1-3
VICIOUS LOYALTY 1-3
By **Kingpen**

THE ULTIMATE SACRIFICE 1-6
KHADIFI
IF YOU CROSS ME ONCE 1-3
ANGEL 1-4
IN THE BLINK OF AN EYE
By **Anthony Fields**

THE LIFE OF A HOOD STAR
By **Ca$h & Rashia Wilson**

NIGHTMARES OF A HUSTLA 1-3
BLOOD AND GAMES 1&2
By **King Dream**

GHOST MOB
By **Stilloan Robinson**

186

HARD AND RUTHLESS 1&2
MOB TOWN 251
THE BILLIONAIRE BENTLEYS 1-3
REAL G'S MOVE IN SILENCE
By **Von Diesel**

MOB TIES 1-7
SOUL OF A HUSTLER, HEART OF A KILLER 1-3
GORILLAZ IN THE TRENCHES
By **SayNoMore**

BODYMORE MURDERLAND 1-3
THE BIRTH OF A GANGSTER 1-4
By **Delmont Player**

FOR THE LOVE OF A BOSS 1&2
By **C. D. Blue**

KILLA KOUNTY 1-5
By **Khufu**

MOBBED UP 1-4
THE BRICK MAN 1-5
THE COCAINE PRINCESS 1-10
STEPPERS 1-3
SUPER GREMLIN 1-4
By **King Rio**

MONEY GAME 1&2
By **Smoove Dolla**

A GANGSTA'S KARMA 1-4
By **FLAME**

KING OF THE TRENCHES 1-3
By **GHOST & TRANAY ADAMS**

COUNTDOWN OF A KILLA 2 | LO-LIFE

QUEEN OF THE ZOO 1&2
By **Black Migo**

GRIMEY WAYS 1-3
BETRAYAL OF A G
By **Ray Vinci**

XMAS WITH AN ATL SHOOTER
By **Ca$h & Destiny Skai**

KING KILLA 1&2
By **Vincent "Vitto" Holloway**

BETRAYAL OF A THUG 1&2
By **Fre$h**

THE MURDER QUEENS 1-5
By **Michael Gallon**

FOR THE LOVE OF BLOOD 1-4
By **Jamel Mitchell**

HOOD CONSIGLIERE 1&2
NO TIME FOR ERROR
By **Keese**

PROTÉGÉ OF A LEGEND 1&2
LOVE IN THE TRENCHES 1&2
By **Corey Robinson**

THE PLUG'S RUTHLESS DAUGHTER
By **Tony Daniels**

BORN IN THE GRAVE 1-3
CRIME PAYS
By **Self Made Tay**

MOAN IN MY MOUTH
By **XTASY**

TORN BETWEEN A GANGSTER AND A GENTLEMAN
By **J-BLUNT & Miss Kim**

LOYALTY IS EVERYTHING 1-3
CITY OF SMOKE 1&2
By **Molotti**

HERE TODAY GONE TOMORROW 1&2
By **Fly Rock**

WOMEN LIE MEN LIE 1-4
FIFTY SHADES OF SNOW 1-3
STACK BEFORE YOU SPLURGE
GIRLS FALL LIKE DOMINOES
NAÏVE TO THE STREETS
By **ROY MILLIGAN**

PILLOW PRINCESS
By **S. Hawkins**

THE BUTTERFLY MAFIA 1-3
SALUTE MY SAVAGERY 1&2
By **Fumiya Payne**

THE LANE 1&2
By Ken-Ken Spence

THE PUSSY TRAP 1-5
By **Nene Capri**

DIRTY DNA
By **Blaque**

SANCTIFIED AND HORNY
by **XTASY**

BOOKS BY LDP'S CEO, CA$H

TRUST IN NO MAN
TRUST IN NO MAN 2
TRUST IN NO MAN 3
BONDED BY BLOOD
SHORTY GOT A THUG
THUGS CRY
THUGS CRY 2
THUGS CRY 3
TRUST NO BITCH
TRUST NO BITCH 2
TRUST NO BITCH 3
TIL MY CASKET DROPS
RESTRAINING ORDER
RESTRAINING ORDER 2
IN LOVE WITH A CONVICT
LIFE OF A HOOD STAR
XMAS WITH AN ATL SHOOTER

www.ingramcontent.com/pod-product-compliance
Lightning Source LLC
Chambersburg PA
CBHW070516260626
47161CB00004B/1566